ESPECIALLY FOR GIRLS™ *presents*

Some Other Summer

By C. S. ADLER

MACMILLAN PUBLISHING CO., Inc.

New York

ACKNOWLEDGMENTS:

With thanks for the expert help of Linda Walmet who corrected the material dealing with horses in this book.

And with special thanks to Oscar Schwerdtfeger who shared his experiences fighting fires as a volunteer fireman in Putnam Station, New York, through a vividly written ten-page letter that I used as the background for one of the final chapters.   —C. S. A.

Library of Congress Cataloging in Publication Data
Adler, C. S. (Carole S.)
Some other summer.

Summary: A thirteen-year-old orphan is
baffled and upset when her long-time friend
Jeremy comes to spend the summer on her uncle's
horse ranch and seems to ignore her. Continues
the story of "The Magic of the Glits."
[1. Orphans—Fiction.   2. Horses—Fiction.
3. Ranch life—Fiction]   I. Title.
PZ7.A26145So   1982   [Fic]   82–7161
ISBN 0–02–700290–X   AACR2

Some Other Summer

Chapter 1

Just as Lynette started grooming her copper-colored mare, Penny, a black spider as big as a saucer swung down and stopped right next to Penny's eye. The mare snorted with surprise. Suddenly the narrow stall became a trap. A thousand pounds of rearing horse left nowhere for Lynette to go but against the wall as flat as she could press herself. Whinnying in fear, the mare slammed her forefeet down.

"It's all right, Penny. Don't be scared," Lynette said to calm her. "It's just a spider. It won't hurt you."

Penny backed against the half door of her stall, which bowed out with her weight. The wood screamed ominously.

"Whoa, whoa, Penny," Lynette pleaded. She was afraid the horse might kick the door out. Uncle Josh already had more repairs to do than he had time for. "Look, the spider's gone. It's disappeared." It was true. The spider seemed to have retreated as suddenly as it came. Lynette didn't suspect anything until she heard a giggle over the heavy breathing of the nervous horse. It came from the empty stall next door. Wrapping her arms around Penny's neck, Lynette yelled, "Who's there?...Eddie?" The sound of footsteps sent her dashing out of Penny's stall in time to tackle the slower of the two escaping boys. She brought Eddie down onto the dirty floor of the barn.

"Eddie Michael John Barber! That was the worst trick you ever played on me."

"No, no. Let go of me, Lynette. I didn't do nothing."

She sat astride her nine-year-old cousin. He was four years younger than she and the only person on the ranch smaller and skinnier than she was. She pinned his arms so he couldn't shake her off. "What were you doing in that stall, then?" she demanded.

"Nothing. Just hiding with Milton."

"To spy on me?"

"How we gonna do that? The wall's too high."

"When it comes to spying, you find a way."

The half wall between stalls was certainly over Eddie's head, but he might have gotten a boost up from Milton, who was a hefty kid. All at once, Lynette realized where that spider had come from. "Don't you know it's dangerous to tease a horse in a stall like that? She could've kicked me or hurt herself."

"You're always picking on me, Lynette," Eddie whimpered.

"That's a lie!" She was outraged. Eddie would say anything to get out of trouble. She could never pin a truth on him that he didn't squirm out from under. "You promise never to do a thing like that to Penny again," Lynette threatened.

"A little menace is what you are. *You're* the one picks on me. Why are you so mean to me, Eddie? You don't bug Debbi half as much as you do me," said Lynette.

"Debbi's mean," Eddie said. "She don't care about nothing no more except her boyfriends."

"Are you going to promise?"

2

"You going to smack me?"

"I'll tell Uncle Josh what you did."

"Josh ain't gonna do nothing to me," Eddie boasted.

Lynette bit her lip. He was right about his father. All Josh ever did was laugh at Eddie's mischief. He never disciplined this youngest of his string of six children. "All right, then," Lynette said. "I'll speak to Marie. She won't let you get away with doing anything to horses."

"I'm not scared of her. What's Marie gonna do to me? She's not my mother anyways. Josh only married her so's she could take care of his horses."

"Eddie." Lynette softened at the whine of loneliness coming through in his voice. She knew what it was like to miss a mother. "Why can't you be nice to me like you used to? Remember when you and I were friends in New Mexico? Remember how you used to sit in my lap and I'd tell you stories?"

"I don't act like a baby no more. I'm big now." He struggled to get loose. "Let me go, Lynette. Milton's waiting for me."

"Soon as you promise."

"I promise."

"What?"

"That I won't be mean to your sway-backed old nag."

She sighed, and let him up.

"Just to you," he finished. With a triumphant laugh, he darted out the door. Useless to follow him; he was quick as a lizard. She heard the mocking giggle of sleepy-eyed Milton as Eddie joined his waiting partner and the two boys ran off together. Milton was even more hateful that Eddie. Milton lacked a whole brain. Of course, that didn't keep Eddie from inviting him over all the time and showing off for him as if Milton were someone special.

Lynette stood up. She'd let Eddie get away with it again.

3

Dealing with him was so frustrating. Maybe Jeremy would help her. Jeremy was seventeen. He'd know what to do with a slippery little brat like Eddie.

To calm herself, Lynette breathed deeply of the barn smell which she loved, the rich mix of manure and sweet hay and warm animals. The barn was empty now. Marie had most of the horses out on the trail. Trail rides were the main money-making operation of this ranch Josh had bought in upstate New York. Summer people from houses tucked away in the woods around the lake shore and also some of the motel crowd from the lower end of the lake near the village came to ride. Penny would have been out on the trail today, too, if Jeremy weren't coming. She'd be carrying some small, scared girl who needed a gentle horse. It had been nice of Marie to give Penny the day off.

Lynette hastened back to Penny's stall. So much remained to do before Jeremy's bus came in at four o'clock. Besides making her horse beautiful, Lynette had to transform the house and herself. The pretty blouse Debbi had outgrown and given to her was hanging on the back line waiting to be ironed. Lynette had never had a reason to wear it until today.

Back in Penny's stall, Lynette stared into the speckled sun rays slanting through the barn window. She leaned her cheek against her horse's and let her indignation slowly dissolve. Today she had no time for anything but joy. "Jeremy's coming," she murmured to Penny. "Jeremy's coming. He's coming. He's coming. He's coming at last." She had an urge to caper about and scream out loud. Instead, she picked up the currycomb and forced herself back to work.

Next to Jeremy, Lynette loved Penny more than anybody, except maybe her Uncle Josh. Never mind that the horse was sway-backed and old. She had a gentle disposition and a beautiful head whose Arabian ancestry showed in the delicate bones, lifted nostrils and large, intelligent eyes. Penny *was* intelligent. She understood everything Lynette confided in her. At least, she wrinkled her lips and raised her eyelids and snuffled as if she did.

Penny bumped her moleskin-soft nose affectionately against Lynette's bare arm as Lynette explained, "You and Jeremy will be good friends even if he can't ride you because you're so small, and he wrote that *he's* six feet tall now. But you'll like him because he's the most wonderful boy in the world."

When she was finished with the currycomb, Lynette stroked Penny's coppery hide with the dandy brush, keeping the metal-bristled dog brush ready to use on black mane and tail. The mare looked back at her with hay sticking out of her mouth like scraggly whiskers. Lynette smiled and scolded her affectionately. "Stop fooling with that hay, Penny, and pay attention now." But then she didn't continue speaking. She worked in silence, thinking about the last time she had seen Jeremy.

It was three years ago. She'd been invited to stay with his family and him in Boston for one brief weekend when Josh was moving them from New Mexico to New York. It hadn't been such a good weekend. She had been too shy to talk to Jeremy properly. But now it would be different. She was almost thirteen, and he was coming to spend this summer on the ranch to work for Uncle Josh in exchange for his room and board. That would give Jeremy and her time enough to get to know one another again, and they would become close, better than brother and sister, the way they had been the summer after her mother died when they'd first met.

That summer he'd been so good to her. He'd driven off her loneliness and taught her not to be afraid. But all she'd had of him since, besides that one brief weekend that didn't work, were letters, one of his to every five or six of hers. His letters always began with an apology for not having written more often. Of course, she understood. He was seventeen now and busy with school, his sports, his after-school jobs, his friends. But always she had wished for a miracle to bring him back to her, and now it had happened. Today, he was coming.

She led the well-groomed Penny into the paddock area where the only green on the dry, stamped earth was the burdocks growing fiercely by the fence. Their broad green leaves were indestructible. Time to muck out Penny's stall again. Lynette got the pitchfork and the rake.

Before she left the barn, she made a quick search of the empty stall next to Penny's. Sure enough, the black spider was lying on the floor, real except for its unnatural stillness. Lynette picked it up and angrily ripped off its rubber legs. She tossed the pieces outside the big sliding doors. Criminal to deliberately scare a horse. Eddie ought to be punished. Josh ought to punish him. But suppose Josh lost his temper instead of laughing it off. Sometimes he reacted that way. Better not to rile him now. Eddie was no doubt done with mischief for the day.

Before she headed for the house, Lynette opened the gate to the hilly, rock-strewn pasture to let Penny through. No matter that Penny would undo all the careful grooming by rolling on the muddy ground, tufted with grass, down by the brook. On her day off, Penny deserved to relax instead of being confined just so she'd stay clean for Jeremy. The first time Jeremy saw her, Penny would be standing in the far corner of the pasture under her favorite apple tree. The apple tree was the only one left below the long outcropping of rock fuzzed over with green and gray lichen and surrounded by the low-growing juniper that Josh despised. He said all that picturesque rock and gray-green juniper were signs of poor soil. Rocky hillside and skimpy pasture stretched as far as Lynette could see from the barn.

She crossed the main road to the steep mountainside where Josh had built the small log house they lived in. He'd perched it high above the roadway and dug in a staircase of flat rocks mounting up to it. He took pride in his stonework. He was proudest of all of the enormous stone fireplace in the house that went up like a huge tree from the basement, narrowing through two floors until it poked through the roof at last. Tonight he'd show Jeremy that fireplace, no doubt. She hoped Jeremy appreciated Josh. Josh was such a good-natured man, even though Debbi complained that he didn't have any business sense and would feed a stranger and let his own children go hungry. Debbi hadn't meant Lynette when she had said that about strangers, though. Lynette had asked her and Debbi had said, "You're not a stranger; you're like my sister."

Lynette stood in the doorway and surveyed the living room with dismay. It looked like a garbage dump. What would Jeremy think? He came from a regular family who lived orderly lives. Here on the ranch, the only routines had to do with the horses and their care. Humans had to manage as best they could. Debbi was supposed to be the housekeeper. She'd chosen to keep house instead of working in the barn, but she was easygoing like her father and never let her duties get in the way of her socializing. Besides, she was gone for the week, off on a vacation with a friend.

There was so much to do Lynette didn't know where to start. Luckily the living room was small. The fireplace with its chunky rocks formed one side, and the kitchen area, where an outsized table pushed toward the front door, formed the other. Lynette began collecting the newspapers and torn comics scattered over the floor. All the bowls of partly eaten snacks had to be disposed of, along with the half-empty soda cans left on the arms of the couch and near the cushions on the floor where they'd sprawled last night to watch TV.

7

Washing dishes at the sink, she noted that the clock overhead was strung with spider webs. Jeremy would think he'd come to a pigpen. The fat white cat who slept all day had burrowed into the pile of clean wash which was dumped on the couch awaiting either use of folding, whichever happened first. Ants were already at the sugar Eddie had spilled on the big table. Most disgusting were the dead flies around the windowsills and on the floor where the hot-air ducts were. Lynette swept up the flies and the sugar spill, washed off the sticky kitchen counter that ran between the sink and the stove. She stacked the newspapers into a neat pile beside the fireplace, dispossessed the cat, and was folding up the wash when Eddie poked his impudent face around the corner of the front door. It was the only entrance to the house.

"You still mad at me?" Eddie asked. His bright eyes were sly.

"I found that spider you scared Penny with."

"That's Milton's spider. You better give it back."

"No way! Eddie, don't you understand how bad what you did was?"

I won't do it again," he said easily. "Can you make me some tuna fish?"

"Not today. I'm too busy."

"I said I was sorry." His lower lip rolled down at the corners. The most irritating thing about Eddie was that he never believed himself in the wrong no matter what he did.

"There isn't any tuna fish, anyway," she said. "You fed the last can to the cat."

"Well, then make me peanut butter and bananas."

"Make it yourself."

"Anyway, it was Milton's idea to use the spider."

"You always say it was Milton's idea. If he's such a bad kid, why do you play with him?"

"Because he's my only friend."

8

The answer darted right through Lynette's defenses. Neither of her school friends lived nearby. She knew about making do with whatever companionship was around. "Will you swear you'll never do anything like that to Penny and me again?" she asked Eddie.

"Maybe . . . if you make me a sandwich."

"You're an impossible brat," she said. "You promise, or you won't get anything from me."

"O.K.," he said, but when he turned to go flick on the TV, she saw he had his fingers crossed behind his back to deny the promise. She had already taken the peanut butter down from the cupboard.

"You crossed your fingers! No sandwich," she said.

"Ha, ha, ha!" he said, tensing to run. "Who wants peanut butter anyways."

She lunged at him, but he skittered out the front door, as wary as a housefly in danger of being swatted. She was angry enough to try chasing him. He couldn't escape her around the house unless he clawed his way up the rock ledges or raced down the stone steps to the road. He made for the clothesline next to the tiny vegetable garden Josh had gouged out in the only sunny area that was reasonably level. Her freshly washed blouse had the clothesline all to itself. Eddie yanked the blouse loose and trailed it behind him through the spindly garden.

"Give me that, Eddie," Lynette screeched, so furious that she caught up with him. She grabbed for her blouse. He hung on tightly. "Let go," she ordered. He wouldn't. The ripping sound stunned her. The blouse had torn straight up the back.

"I hate you, you horrible brat," she wailed. His eyes filled with tears. He loped off. He wasn't sassing her now. She didn't care. He deserved the scolding, for the blouse, for Penny, for everything he always got away with with her. She

9

looked at the blouse. Ruined, utterly and forever ruined. Jeremy hadn't seen her for three years, and now she had nothing pretty to wear for him. She dragged herself back indoors.

Upstairs, she threw herself down on her bed in the room she and Debbi shared. If only Debbi weren't on vacation. But even if she were here, it wouldn't matter. She'd be busy getting ready for a date with her boyfriend or talking on the phone. Debbi didn't want to stay inside with the family any more. She was removing herself from them the way her four big brothers had. Only Eddie was still inside, Eddie and Josh and Marie and Lynette. But they didn't make a family. Eddie was too hateful, and Marie was too distant. Marie wasn't comfortable except around horses. Josh was too busy and careless—and she? She didn't really belong to anyone except maybe to Jeremy. She closed her eyes for just a moment to try to recapture her joy. "Jeremy's coming," she said to herself just before sleep overtook her.

Chapter **2**

In the twilight between sleep and waking, she heard Jeremy's voice. I'm dreaming, she thought. She couldn't have slept the whole afternoon. It couldn't be after four already. She sat up and blinked at the shimmering sunlight gilding the dingy, unpainted wallboard around the window. No more than two. The golden glow reminded Lynette of the guest room she had slept in at Jeremy's house on that one weekend in Boston three years ago. That golden room with its furry white bedspread had been the only part of her weekend with Jeremy that hadn't gone wrong. He had tried. He had taken her to the science museum on the subway and showed her a fat albino porcupine there. He had treated her to a movie and asked her how she was doing. It wasn't his fault that she'd been too tangled up with feelings then to talk to him.

"Are you glad your uncle is moving you back East?" Jeremy had asked.

"I don't know." She hadn't yet seen the ranch on Lake George to which they were moving.

"Well, will you miss New Mexico?"

"I don't know."

"How about his new wife? Don't tell me you don't know whether you're glad about *her* or not." He smiled to show he was teasing, but all Lynette could do was stare at him. Her whole life was changing shape around her the way it had after her mother died. She didn't know what would happen except that everything would be different again.

After her aunt, Josh's first wife, walked out on the family in New Mexico, Lynette had been too busy to think about herself. Eddie, who was only five then, had turned to her for comforting. He missed his mama. Even Debbi, two years older than Lynette but less experienced in loss, had needed consolation. Debbi had been angry and confused. And Josh had unsettled them even more by admitting they were close to going broke. Then Marie came to work at the ranch. Soon after that, Josh announced that thanks to Marie, who was a working fool and knew more about horses than anyone he'd ever known, things were looking up.

But before they had time to get familiar with their new relationships, Josh sold the ranch in New Mexico and bought another in upstate New York near Lake George where he had grown up. Just as suddenly, he married Marie. She was a silent woman with a long face and nose, little eyes and calloused hands. She'd never been married and was twenty years younger than Josh. She acted as polite and distant with Josh's kids as if they were strangers. Lynette wasn't able to tell how Marie felt about acquiring a live-in niece along with all Josh's own children.

"Can't you talk to me, Lynette?" Jeremy had asked her in that brief two-day time together when she was ten and he was fifteen. She couldn't. She'd wanted more than anything to tell him how she dreamed of him and longed to be with him, but she couldn't talk to him at all. She had too much to say, too much she was scared about. There had never been another visit after that one, either, not until today.

"Lynette, you up there?" Josh's baritone rang deep and slow. "You got a visitor."

She rolled off the bed to her feet. It *was* Jeremy's voice, then. Josh must have gone to the bus station to pick him up. Oh, why hadn't he taken her with him? She ran to the high, narrow dresser with the mirror above it that was set just right for Debbi who was tall, but too high for Lynette to see anything below her nose. Round, dark eyes fringed with thick, black lashes stared at her as she brushed her shiny hair with quick strokes of the pink plastic hairbrush. Debbi said she was pretty. If only Jeremy would think she was! Too late now to fuss about clothes. She skimmed down the stairs, which curled like a snail shell around the massive stone fireplace, and stopped short three steps from the bottom.

"Jeremy!" she whispered when she saw him. Her heart swelled with love. He and Josh were standing beside the barn-beam mantel. Josh had embedded a piece of tree trunk in the wall above the mantel. The trunk had grown around a horseshoe which stuck out of it curiously. Old medicine bottles Josh had found and jugs and animal traps were fixed in the mortar between the heavy stones so that the fireplace was like a museum wall of farm artifacts.

"It's really amazing," Jeremy said to Josh. "Some wall!"

He'd grown so handsome. Six feet tall now, just as he'd written. The steady gray eyes were the same and the wave of light brown hair over his forehead, but his nose and chin jutted more. He looked so grown up that she was awed. She wanted to run and hug him, but she didn't dare. She had to get reacquainted first.

Just then Eddie bounced into the living room and grabbed Jeremy's attention. "Hi," Eddi said. "Are you Lynette's boyfriend?"

"Hi," came the answer. "I'm Jeremy. And who are you?"

"This is Eddie," Josh said. "My little caboose. He's a

rascal, this one." Josh bent from his burly height and swung Eddie up onto his massive shoulders.

"Looks like someone smacked you good, Eddie. They left their hand print on your face," Jeremy said.

"Lynette hit me," Eddie said. "I didn't do nothing to her. She just hit me for no reason."

"Well, now I doubt that," Josh said, but Jeremy had heard Lynette's gasp and turned to see her on the stairs.

"Lynette," he said. "There you are!"

"I didn't hit him for no reason," she protested, in torment at the ruination of this long-awaited moment.

"What did he do to you?" Jeremy asked.

She barely noticed his smile through the tears in her eyes. "He tore my blouse," she said. "And he—" It was awful. It was terrible. She sounded so mean and childish. She choked on the rest of her own defense.

"This boy's a terrible tease, always giving the girls a hard time, aren't you, tiger?" Josh said to his son.

"She tore her blouse herself," Eddie said. His pixie face was a mask of innocence. "'Cause she wouldn't let go."

"And he scared my horse," Lynette said.

"Milton did. Not me. You hit me for nothing." Eddie slid from his father's shoulder to the floor and took hold of Jeremy's arm. "Where are you gonna bunk, Jeremy? You can bunk in my room with me or else you got to sleep in the basement where my brothers sleep when they visit."

"I'll bunk with you if you want me to," Jeremy said, giving his smile to Eddie.

"O.K. I'll take your pack up, then." Eddie put his arms through the dangling shoulder straps of the green backpack standing beside the door and tried to hoist the pack onto his own narrow frame. He nearly fell over backward, and both the men laughed. Playing up to them, Eddie gritted his teeth and stumbled to the stairs.

"Hey, feller, that's too big for you," Jeremy said.

"No, it isn't." Eddie turned and began backing up the stairs, hauling the backpack after him.

"A real cute kid," Jeremy said to Josh, who rubbed his hand over his own bristly gray hair and nodded. Josh looked young despite his seamed face and work-hardened body. His face radiated such good spirits that people always liked him. Lynette suspected Jeremy already did, but why did he have to be so taken in by Eddie? The little brat was stealing Jeremy from right under her nose by convincing him that *she* was the mean one.

"I wanted to meet you at the bus," Lynette said, hurrying to change his impression of her.

"Don't blame me, honey," Josh said. "He didn't let nobody pick him up, just walked up here on his own."

"I got a ride most of the way and walked the rest," Jeremy said. "Got in earlier than I expected."

"Lynette's been hopping like a grasshopper ever since you wrote you was coming," Josh told him. "If you're half the fellow she claims, you're gonna be a big help to me." His two-day growth of grizzled whiskers rose to meet his twinkling blue eyes as he smiled.

"I'm ready to start working any time," Jeremy said. "I don't know much but I'll try anything."

"Good. Good. I'm gonna put you to the test right off. Our first project is to dig out the spring. All you need's a strong back."

"Strong back, empty head, that's me," Jeremy said cheerfully.

"We'll start tomorrow morning, then. Right now, I suspect you and Lynny here got some catching up to do," Josh said. "So I'll get back to the barn and see you at supper." He held out his hand and Jeremy shook it. Lynette was grateful to Josh. She slipped over to Jeremy and took possession of his other hand. She needed to touch him to believe he was really here at last.

"Will you come meet Penny?" she asked, staring up at him to fix the way he looked now over the old images she had in her mind.

"I got your pack up to the room," Eddie said, reappearing at the bottom of the stairs.

"You're a pretty tough kid," Jeremy thanked him by saying. "Strong for your size."

"I'm tough," Eddie agreed. "I can jump and climb better than Milton."

"Who's Milton?"

"Jeremy, are you coming with me?" Lynette demanded, tugging at him.

"O.K., see you later, kid," Jeremy said and punched Eddie's arm lightly.

"I'll come, too," Eddie said.

"No, you won't." Lynette glared at him. "You watch your television show. It's on soon." She dragged Jeremy out of the house. For once, Eddie did as he was told. But though Jeremy didn't say anything, Lynette suspected she hadn't improved his opinion of the way she treated Eddie any.

"This is some place," Jeremy said, stopping at the top of the steep stone steps to look around. His gaze swung from the pine-furred mountain blocking their view on the left, across the road to the bare, rocky pastures spreading up and away from the barns, and around to the rock ledges scarring the mountain at their right all the way to where the road curved out of sight. "I had no idea New York State had country this rugged."

"It's very green, isn't it?" Lynette said. She had preferred the sunburned bareness of the desert where the sky went on forever. The greenness here oppressed her.

"You ever do any mountain-climbing?" Jeremy asked,

following her down the wide rock steps.

"No, there's no time. We have to take care of the horses."

"Yeah, I guess there's plenty to keep everybody busy on a ranch," Jeremy said.

"Especially this ranch," Lynette explained. "Josh says it's a poor, rundown place, and we have to make up in work for what we don't have in money."

"If it's that bad, why doesn't he get rid of it and get a job working for someone else?"

"Josh says it's not in his nature to work for anyone else."

"What happens if he can't make a go of it here, then?" Jeremy asked.

"We sell off horses," Lynette said grimly. She thought of those painful times when Marie had singled out horses to sell because they couldn't afford the high feed bills over the winter. Marie's plain, long-jawed face would stretch out with misery. She'd ignore Josh's fumbling attempts to cheer her up and spend even more hours of her long day out in the barns, giving extra attention to those horses marked for sale. When the big horse vans rumbled to a stop on the road next to the barn, Marie would look as if she were dying.

"Is that so terrible?" Jeremy asked. "To sell off horses?"

"Yes. Most of the horses we have, nobody wants—not for pets or anything decent. Most of the horses here Marie's rescued from the slaughterhouse. That's where they go if we have to sell them again."

"That really bothers you, huh?"

"Yes," she said. She thought of her nightmare. Sometimes there was a dark, rocking van jammed with frightened horses and sometimes she was there in the van with them. When she wakened screaming, Debbi would get into bed with her to comfort her, but usually before Lynette could even tell Debbi what the dream had been about, Debbi would fall asleep again, and Lynette would have to comfort herself.

17

"Don't be foolish," she'd say aloud. "Don't be foolish." Josh would not get rid of her even if she was only his niece and not his own child.

"Lynette," Jeremy said. "Don't look so sad. Maybe it'll never happen again. Maybe Josh will make a mint this summer."

"Maybe," she said.

"You know something," Jeremy went on. "You're looking good. You're growing up pretty."

She flushed with pleasure, but pushed away the compliment by saying, "I'm not as pretty as Debbi."

"Your cousin? The one you wrote me all the boys like?"

"Debbi's the only other girl around here besides me. She'll be back in a week. Her girlfriend took her along to the Finger Lakes on their family's vacation. Josh let her go even though he really needs all the hands he can get." This time he wouldn't think she couldn't talk to him. This time she would tell him everything.

"Why'd he let her go, then?"

"Josh can't say no to his kids."

"How about to you?"

She hesitated. Then she said carefully, "I never ask him for anything."

"What do you mean? Why not?"

"Well, because he's already doing more for me than he needs to do just keeping me. Josh is a good man."

"Yeah, he seems like a nice guy."

They walked to the gate of the wood and wire fence which surrounded the pasture and stood there a minute. Jeremy said, "You've changed a lot. You never used to be a fighter. Do you fight with your girl cousin, too?"

"Fight with Debbi? What for? What do you mean?"

"The way you fight with Eddie. You used to be the gentlest little girl."

There it was! Now he thought she was a brute.

"Eddie lied," she defended herself hotly. "I had good reason to hit him. I told you."

"Hey, take it easy. Don't get so upset. All I mean is hitting a child doesn't help anything."

"You don't understand, Jeremy. He scared my horse and he—"

"If a child needs punishing," he interrupted her, "you can do it without hitting him." He put his foot up on the gate and started telling her about a bad kid at the camp where he'd worked last summer. She heard his voice but not the actual words. She couldn't believe that he was talking to her this way—as if she were not a good person. Here he was standing next to her and there was Penny browsing under the apple tree making a postcard-perfect picture, the very stuff of half her daydreams, but Jeremy didn't seem to see Penny, and Lynette's feelings were all wrong, too. ". . . so what I learned," Jeremy was saying, "is that a child responds best to love."

"Please, Jeremy," she begged and touched his arm urgently. "Let's not talk about Eddie any more." She would make a new start, now, this minute, before any more misunderstandings came between them.

He shrugged. "Whatever you say."

She pointed at Penny who was busy flicking horseflies off with her long, flowing black tail, so long it hung all the way down to her hocks. "That's Penny."

"Your horse? That one with the caved-in middle?" He sounded amused.

"Penny's beautiful," Lynette said sharply and frowned at him.

"Hey," he said. "Hey, I didn't mean to hurt your feelings. She's a nice-looking horse, pretty color, anyway."

Lynette whistled. Penny lifted her head. With ears perked

daintily, she trotted down the hill and put her head over the fence, ready to be sociable.

"See, she's voice-trained," Lynette said. "I don't even need reins to guide her."

"Uh huh. That's nice. I guess she's special all right." He didn't sound sincere.

Penny snorted softly. Lynette said, "She was starving when Marie got her. Most of the horses we have Marie saved and built up, but not too many turn out as wonderful as Penny." Lynette wrapped her arms around Penny's neck and in a muffled voice said to Jeremy, "I'm not a mean person like Eddie said."

"I know you're not," Jeremy said. "Say, we're old buddies, aren't we? Don't I know what you're like?"

He looked so tall and different. Did he know? Did he really know her any more? She wanted to hear him say he'd come to be with her this summer. She wanted to hear all the words he never put in letters because boys didn't write mushy things, like how special she was to him and how much he cared about her, but he had to care. Otherwise, why had he come?

"Do you remember the summer when my stepfather left me at your house in Cape Cod, Jeremy?"

"Sure I do," he said. "I remember the first time I ever saw you."

"You do?"

"Uh huh. You were sitting in a chair in the living room looking sad. I took you down to the beach and we built a sand castle."

"And you told me wonderful stories and played with me. You were so good to me, Jeremy."

"Well, sure, you were just a little kid and you'd lost your mother. I felt sorry for you."

"And you saved my life," she said.

"I didn't do anything. You did it yourself. *You* wrote to your uncle to ask him to take you in. That was pretty smart for a seven-year-old kid."

She let him talk and tell her how it had been. He didn't guess how fiercely she had loved him or that she loved him still. He didn't know that someday she meant to grow up and marry him. She let him talk and wondered when she could ask him to wait for her. She had so far to go until she was a woman, and now she could see that he'd become a man already. Why did he have to jump so far ahead of her? She let him talk and went on dreaming. She would grow up fast and Jeremy would wait for her.

Chapter 3

Every morning that week, before Lynette got back from helping Marie tack up the horses for the trail rides and muck out the stalls that had been used overnight, Jeremy and Josh would have eaten breakfast and gone off to dig out the spring. Josh wanted to lay pipe underground so that the water to the barn wouldn't freeze again as it had last winter. Midday, Lynette saw Jeremy at lunch. Then she would report such items as the deer she had startled while riding through the upper pasture. "Couldn't you come riding with me tomorrow, Jeremy?" she would ask.

"If I have time," he would answer and go on to joke about the gold he had found in the brook. "I was so excited. Didn't you hear me yelling, 'Gold, gold!'? I thought we'd struck it rich—until Josh told me it was just shiny pyrite."

Late afternoons when Josh quit working and took off in the truck on errands, Jeremy sometimes went with him. Lynette would be cooling down horses back from the trail rides and seeing to their feed and water buckets, and she'd hear the truck roar off down the road. At suppertime, she tried to please Jeremy with dishes he might like, but he never noticed what he ate.

"I got enough appetite from working for this old slave-driver uncle of yours so I could fill up on horse feed and not know the difference," Jeremy told her.

"Working you hard, am I?" Josh asked.

"You'll either kill me or make a man of me, Josh."

"What are you doing it for, then, if it's so hard?" Lynette asked.

"Look at Josh's muscles," Jeremy said. "That's what I'm doing it for, to get muscles like his."

Josh roared, pleased by Jeremy's admiration, and whacked him on the back. Jeremy pretended to be bowled over and fell on the floor gasping. When Eddie ran to his side, thinking his friend was really hurt, Jeremy hid his head against his forearm and moaned, "Don't touch me, Eddie. I'm nothing but a sack of sore bones." He got up quickly enough, though, when Marie said the soup was on the table.

Evenings, Jeremy lay on the floor in front of the TV with his head on a cushion beside Eddie's and promptly fell asleep.

At the end of that first week, Lynette was wondering if she'd ever get any time alone with Jeremy. It was nice to see him daily, but she yearned for long, quiet talks with him. Saturday morning, en route to his captain's chair at the big wooden table, Josh stopped to lay his gnarled hand on Jeremy's shoulder.

"Jeremy, you've earned your keep this week. Am I pushing you too hard?"

"Well, Josh," Jeremy said, "I guess I must be crazy because I have to admit I'm enjoying myself even though you've half killed me."

"That's the spirit, boy. You've got to be crazy to work on a horse ranch. But I'd say you're due for a break. Why don't you and Lynette grab a couple of horses and head for the hills today? Some pretty country up there she should show you."

Marie looked up from her usual breakfast of fried eggs and toast and said, "Don't someone have to pick up Debbi later? She's due back today."

"Well," Josh considered, "how's about you and me doing that, Marie honey? You haven't been to town in weeks. I guess the ranch won't fall apart if we leave it for a couple of hours."

"You said you were going to look at that break in the barn roof, Josh. And after this morning's trail ride, I've gotta see to the roan gelding. Looks like he's going lame."

"Yeah. . . . And Plunkett's coming about buying that Morgan you been feeding up so good for his daughter. . . . Well, well, it'll all work out. A man, nor a woman neither, can't work round the clock, Marie." He covered her hand with his and squeezed. "Right?"

Marie looked up at him with a wondering smile that sweetened her hard-planed face. The smile faded fast, though. "Got to get moving," she muttered to herself and gulped down her coffee.

"Can I go with you and Lynette, Jer?" Eddie asked. He pushed his half-eaten cereal aside. "Please, can I?" His eagerness was answered by Jeremy's ready smile.

Without consulting Lynette, Jeremy said, "Sure, Eddie."

The joyful rise of anticipation in Lynette sank fast. Finally, she had been going to have Jeremy to herself and now Eddie had to butt in. "You can't keep up with Jeremy and me on your pony, Eddie," she said.

"Why not? Are we in a hurry?" Jeremy asked.

"I'm not riding my pony. I'll ride—Hotspur," Eddie decided. "Josh? Can I ride Hotspur? You said I'm a real good rider now."

"Not good enough to control Hotspur with a feather-weight like you on his back—no," Josh said. "Let's see. What do you think, Marie? Annabelle be O.K. for Eddie?"

"Annabelle," Eddie protested. "That old nag! My pony can go faster than her."

"A girl for this morning's trail asked for Annabelle special. What trail you planning on taking?" Marie asked Lynette.

"Up back of the mountain," Lynette said promptly. She imagined leading Jeremy out from the canopy of tall trees onto the ledge. The view was spectacular across the lake to the dark green mountains hunched shoulder to shoulder on the far side like animals at a watering hole. Some mountains were studded by outcroppings of lichen-mottled rock; some were feathered in shades of green. The shadows of the clouds moving across them made them look alive. Jeremy would love it.

"That trail hasn't been used much this season," Marie said. "Could be some surprises on it."

"We'll be careful," Lynette promised. "It's so pretty, Marie. It's my favorite ride."

Marie smiled at Lynette's eagerness. "O.K.," she said. "But you watch yourself on it."

"Eddie, how'd you like to ride Gypsy?" Josh asked.

"Yeah, wow, Gypsy!"

"She's sure-footed," Josh said to Marie.

"Spirited, though."

"Ed's a good rider."

Marie shrugged. The horses were her responsibility, but it was Eddie's safety that was in question, not the horses', and the children were Josh's concern. Josh managed the business end of the ranch, saw to repairs and raised his own children.

Lynette made one last feeble attempt to keep Eddie out of her party. "Don't you think Debbi will be hurt if you don't help pick her up at the bus stop, Eddie?"

"Uh uh. She won't care."

"Bet Josh would treat you to some candy if you go."

"I wanna go with you and Jer."

Lynette sighed and turned to doing the breakfast dishes. No way to shake him loose. He'd latched onto Jeremy so firmly that even Milton was taking second place. If only Jeremy didn't make such a good big brother! He fooled around with Eddie and answered his endless questions. They were always swatting at and chasing each other, having mock boxing matches or running races. Probably Eddie needed all that. He missed the two youngest of his four older brothers since they'd joined the army. Lynette wished Eddie would switch back to Milton, though.

She cinched the girth around her horse's low-slung belly as tight as she could and told Penny, "We're going to have fun today, and *you're* going to be the lead horse because Jeremy doesn't know the way and I do. Aren't you proud?" Penny raised her lip and showed her teeth in a horse laugh.

Lynette hitched her to the railing in the paddock and went to help the boys tack up. Jeremy had put the bridle on Silver so that the bit was bothering the horse. The big, quiet bay had been Marie's suggestion as a good mount for Jeremy. Jeremy was busy helping Eddie get a saddle on Gypsy. While he wasn't looking, Lynette quietly removed the bridle from Silver and put it on right.

"Up you go," Jeremy said, as he boosted Eddie into the saddle. Eddie looked small as a jockey perched up there on the high horse. Gypsy bowed her neck and tossed her head restlessly as if something bothered her.

"You going to be O.K., Eddie?" Jeremy asked doubtfully.

"Sure, I can handle any horse we got," Eddie boasted.

"His stirrups aren't even," Lynette said. Jeremy held Gypsy's head while Lynette adjusted the left stirrup.

"Is Lynette your girlfriend, Jer?" Eddie asked.

"No. She's too little to be my girlfriend."

"She's too short?" Eddie asked.

"No. Too young," Jeremy said.

"Jeremy and I are old friends," Lynette added.

"No, you're not. He said you're young."

"Oh, Eddie, don't be stupid," Lynette said.

Jeremy laughed. A lot of Eddie's nonsense amused him. She wondered how funny he'd find a soft, cold toad against his bare skin when he slid between the sheets at night, or a pot of water that spilled over when he opened the bedroom door, or Eddie hiding under a bed to spy on him. She didn't think it was so funny when Eddie did those things to her.

"Well, do you have *any* girlfriend?" Eddie asked.

Jeremy swung into his saddle, forgetting to collect his reins first. Lynette handed them to him. "I had one," Jeremy answered, "but she told me to get lost."

"How come?" Eddie asked.

"I don't know. I guess she found a guy she liked better than me. But it worked out O.K. She and I had jobs at the same day camp for this summer, and if she hadn't ditched me, that's where I'd be now instead of here."

"Why didn't you want to work at the day camp?" Eddie asked. "Just because she ditched you?"

"I don't know. I guess I felt bad that she had another guy," Jeremy said.

"Girls always do that," Eddie said.

"Do what?" Jeremy asked.

"They always tell you to get lost."

"Ain't it the truth!" Jeremy chuckled to himself all the way across the pasture to where the trail began.

Chill shock waves kept hitting Lynette as she rode beside him. Jeremy had a girlfriend and she hadn't even known. He never wrote things like that. He could be falling in love and lost to her forever and she would never know. That was bad enough to find out, but even worse was that he'd come here to the ranch this summer as a last resort. He hadn't come to be with her at all.

"Hey, Lynette," Jeremy said, looking down at her from his creaking saddle. "What're you so down in the mouth about?"

"Nothing." How was it possible, she thought, that she could care so much about him and matter so little to him? An imbalance that great just wasn't fair.

Chapter 4

Once they entered the trail through the trees, they had to go single file. Silver kept pushing up alongside Penny's flanks so that his head bumped Lynette's feet. He definitely did not like walking behind Penny in the line-up.

"I think it hurts his pride to follow old Penny," Jeremy said. "Whoa there, Silver. Ladies first. Come on now; take it easy."

Lynette looked over her shoulder and saw Jeremy hauling on the reins without much effect. Silver had a hard mouth and a strong will. Gypsy was lagging behind them. Eddie, too, seemed to be having trouble because Gypsy kept dancing sideways along the trail, tossing her mane. Lynette wondered what was bothering the usually dependable horse.

"Is Eddie going to be O.K. on that horse?" Jeremy murmured to Lynette.

"I don't know," Lynette said, and because she was responsible as the leader she added, "Maybe we should turn back and get his pony."

"But Josh knows what Eddie can handle, doesn't he?" Jeremy said.

They kept going. The old logging road passed through the grabbing vines of the blackberry bushes and branched off, heading up the mountain. The path Lynette chose led them above the gully where, in spring, water racketed down over the stones in a noisy torrent. A trickle still ran by now.

"It's really wild up here," Jeremy said, pulling alongside her.

"Yes," Lynette answered. "It's beautiful, isn't it?" She had meant the beauty to be her gift to him. The gift was still there even if her peace of mind wasn't. Don't think about it, she told herself. Think about today and being with him now.

"Did you bring anything to eat?" Jeremy asked her.

"I made peanut butter and baloney sandwiches and brought Kool-Aid."

"Do you really think peanut butter and baloney taste good together?" Jeremy teased as the saddles squeaked and the horses' bellies bumped, squeezing the riders' legs between them.

"I thought you'd eat anything," she answered back with a smile.

The clop of the horses' hooves and the snap of twigs breaking underfoot were the loudest sounds. In the still air, the tap, tap, tap of a woodpecker digging in the bark of a dead tree for his dinner rang sharply.

"Tell me something, Lynette," Jeremy said. "Are you happy here?"

The question surprised her. "I'm happy now you're here," she said.

"And when I'm not around?"

"Sometimes I'm happy."

"When?"

"When I'm with Penny."

"That's all? Don't you like Josh and your cousins and Marie?"

"Sure I do. I love Josh and Marie's nice and Debbi—" The familiar pang of regret came for all Debbi had been to her.

"So you're basically pretty happy."

She didn't answer him. No way to explain to him how it was to not quite belong, to be always on the anxious edge of things. She wasn't Josh's child. He didn't *have* to feed and clothe and care for her the way he did his own. She depended on his generosity. She thought of the horses that had to be sold when the bills got too high. But she wasn't a horse.

Lynette shivered. There had been that kid in her class in school. Nancy was her name. She had a bad skin condition and glared at everyone. Lynette had befriended her because no one else did, but Lynette didn't have to be her friend for long. Halfway through the term, Nancy had told Lynette she was leaving. Her foster parents were turning her over to the court. "Why?" Lynette had asked.

"Guess they just got sick of having me around," Nancy had said, pretending she didn't care. "I been to the Girls' Home before," she said. "It's not so bad."

Lynette wondered where Josh would send her if he couldn't afford to keep her. She didn't have any other family. Her father had disappeared when she was five. Her mother had drowned when she was seven. She couldn't go to Jeremy, not until she was old enough to marry him.

"Hey, Lynette," Jeremy said. He allowed Silver to nose ahead of Penny. "Know what Josh says about you?"

"No, what?"

"He says you're so smart it scares him. He says you ought to go to college and be a teacher or something."

"Maybe I will."

"I wish I was sure of what I'd be good at."

"You'd be good at anything you want to do, Jeremy."

"Do you think so? Josh doesn't hold out much hope for me as a ditch-digger, and I'm no good with horses, that's for sure. Maybe I'll have more talent for putting in fence posts. We start that next week."

"Jeremy, are you really glad you came?"

"Sure," he said. "I wouldn't have missed this summer with you for anything."

Her heart flew up joyously. That was what she wanted to hear.

The hill hugged them on one side of the steep trail and the mountain closed in on the other. It was dark and cool and moist. They pressed on in silence, back to single-file order with Lynette in the lead, until Jeremy yelled, "Look at that!" Three plump birds flew straight up in a whirr of wings.

"Partridge," Lynette said. She pushed up a tree branch under which Penny had just fitted and handed it back to Jeremy before ducking under herself.

"Should have brought a hatchet for this kind of stuff," Jeremy said. "Are you sure this trail's navigable?" He struggled to break the branch, which was too low for Silver and for him.

"It's worth it when you come out on the ledge," Lynette encouraged him. "You can see for miles up the lake."

"How you doing back there, Eddie?" Jeremy asked.

"Fine. Gypsy likes going uphill," Eddie said.

"Behaving herself now?"

"Yeah, I got her trained good."

Lynette shook her head at Eddie's excess of self-confidence and picked up the reins to help Penny over a tree trunk lying across the path. Silver snorted and leaped the tree trunk, surprising Jeremy.

"Whoops!" Jeremy yelped.

"Silver's a good jumper," Lynette told him, looking back over his shoulder. "Just ease up on the reins, lean forward, and let him take over."

"Suppose I don't want him to jump?"

"Well, I guess you stop him and turn around and go some

32

other way. Otherwise, he'll jump no matter what you do."

She pointed to the side of the gully where water fell from a lip of rock in a twisting silver ribbon which splashed up between the boulders at the bottom. "Isn't it pretty here?"

"Nice," he said.

The path began its curve around the bare rock and moss-covered shoulder of the mountain toward the lake. Now chunks of rocks littered the ground. Lynette wasn't worried. All three horses were sure-footed. Penny patiently picked her way through the debris and finally stepped onto the broad ledge that overlooked the enormous expanse of humped mountains and lake. Lynette dismounted, keeping hold of the reins.

"Wow!" Jeremy said. "It really is something, isn't it?"

They tied the horses to a one-armed tree that had twisted its way up through the rocky ledge as if it, too, were struggling to get to the view. Lynette unpacked the sandwiches and Kool-Aid. The three of them sat down on the flat, sunwarmed stone a few feet back from the edge. Below them was a sheer drop of several hundred feet before the canopy of evergreen, oak and ash and butternut began. The dark green lake was stippled with small sail and motor boats. Even the big paddle wheeler that glided imperiously by, taking sightseers on tour of the lake, looked no bigger than a car from their perch. The mountains on the opposite shore had the rounded contours of old age and were heavily bearded with trees. Their bald spots were smooth rock out-croppings at their crests. The sky was bare of clouds and full of sun.

"Wish we could go swimming," Eddie said.

"Maybe next time we can ride the horses down to the lake," Lynette said. "But Jeremy had to see the view one time at least."

"It's really spectacular," Jeremy said. "I wish I had a camera."

She was happy. She had given him something good. "I'm so glad to be here with you, Jeremy."

He smiled at her and patted her hand. She turned her hand around and squeezed his. I love you, Jeremy, she wanted to say. But before she could say anything, he tugged his hand away.

"Hey, don't do that," he said to Eddie, who was balling his sandwich wrapper and heaving it over the cliff. "That's littering."

"It's just paper," Eddie said.

"Yeah, but you don't want to walk through the woods and find everybody's discarded paper and plastic and cans, do you?"

Eddie considered. "I don't care."

"Well, you will when you get old enough to know better."

"O.K., Jeremy. Can we go back now?" Eddie said.

Lynette sighed. She would have liked to sit a while and enjoy the view and the pleasure of being beside Jeremy, but she didn't object when Jeremy stood up and gave Eddie a hand up onto Gypsy.

To Lynette's amazement, Gypsy reared when Eddie settled down onto the saddle. If he hadn't had such a good grip with his legs, he would have been thrown off immediately. That might have been better. As it was, Gypsy took off running back down the path, out of control, as soon as her front feet touched the ground. Lynette screamed. Penny whinnied. She was ready to chase the runaway as soon as Lynette scrambled into the saddle. Penny trotted down the path as fast as she could safely go, but she refused Lynette's voice commands urging her faster. Lynette kicked Penny's belly sharply with her heels. Penny just whinnied again and tap-tapped her careful way through the rocks.

"Let me by, Lynette," Jeremy said right behind her. "Silver can catch up with them."

"This path's too dangerous to run on."

"Pull to the right, I'm coming through." Silver's head surged past Lynette's waist. He was so much bigger than Penny. Lynette hugged the moss-covered slope and reined Penny in. It was safer to let them go than to try and stop them.

"Be careful, Jeremy!" she called.

If anyone was going to get hurt, let it be her or Eddie, not Jeremy. "Oh, please," she begged as a certainty that something was going to happen swelled painfully in her chest. Silver sailed gracefully over the fallen tree trunk. His big horse-shoe shaped white rump disappeared down the trail. Jeremy jigged awkwardly in the saddle as Silver cantered. His peculiar gait was hard for a rider.

"The branch!" Lynette screamed and kicked Penny so hard that Penny jumped into a canter. Lynette could see Jeremy lying dead on the path in her mind. She put her head down and she and Penny easily passed under the branch. No sign of Jeremy or Eddie yet. That gave her hope. The trail improved from this point on, but just as she was imagining that they might all make it home without mishap, she saw Jeremy standing in the path, leaning over Eddie who was lying face down on the ground. The horses were not in sight. Lynette reined Penny in, slipped off and ran to Jeremy's side.

"He's dead," Jeremy said, horror-struck.

She crouched down and put her ear against Eddie's back. "No, he's not," she said. "Turn him over. You'll see."

"We shouldn't touch him. His bones might be broken."

"Then what are we supposed to do, let him lie here? No one's at the ranch. If his bones are broken, we have to get him to a hospital so he can get x-rayed and all that."

"Right. You're right, Lynette. O.K. Here, help me lift him."

35

Together they lifted Eddie carefully and turned him over. He opened his eyes. Lynette stroked his cheek. "Are you all right, Eddie?"

"I fell off."

"Do you hurt anyplace?"

Abruptly, Eddie sat up. He touched the back of his head with his hand. "Lynette," he whimpered. She put her arms around him and drew him into her lap. Jeremy examined him for broken bones. "I feel funny," Eddie said.

"How funny?"

"My head feels funny."

"Maybe he has a concussion," Jeremy said. "Nothing seems to be broken. I can't believe he doesn't have anything but that scrape on his cheek."

"Lynette, I wanna go home," Eddie said and clung to her as she helped him stand up.

"Do you think you can ride with me?" she asked. "Penny can get us home quick." Quicker then they could make it on foot, anyway. The other horses were probably halfway to the barn by now.

Jeremy lifted Eddie up onto the saddle behind Lynette. Eddie leaned his head against her back and wrapped his arms around her.

"You'll be all right walking back alone?" Lynette asked Jeremy.

"Sure, no problem. I'm just glad nothing too bad happened. We could've had a disaster."

Lynette nodded. "We were lucky." She wondered, as Penny plodded slowly homeward, what had gotten into Gypsy. She was a spirited horse normally, but well-behaved. Marie had better take a look at her.

No one was at the barns. The pickup was parked by the stairs. Lynette left Penny in the paddock and half dragged, half walked Eddie across the road and up to the house. She could hear Debbi's ringing laugh all the way up the steps.

"Eddie had an accident," Lynette said when she stumbled in with Eddie in tow. "He fell off Gypsy." It was a relief to hand him over to Josh, who always knew what to do in an emergency. Josh carried Eddie into the downstairs bedroom. If there was anything wrong with Eddie's head, Josh would see to it. Lynette told Marie about Gypsy's peculiar behavior. Then she said hello to Debbi, who stood there calmly, looking as terrific as ever with her broad shoulders and narrow hips and long legs and long blond hair. She had a fresh, country-girl face. Everything about her was strong and direct.

"Did you have a good time?" Lynette asked her.

"Great, except I could have done with a lot less of all that car travel. It's boring spending six hours at a shot in a car. But we saw a lot of stuff and Helen and I met some cute guys."

"On a traveling vacation?"

"Why not? One of them says he'll write to me. He goes to college in Albany. That's not far."

"I'm going to take care of Penny. Want to come out to the barn with me and talk?" Lynette asked.

"Not really. I've still got to unpack. We can talk when you're done. Your Jeremy's here, I understand. Is he cute?"

"You'll see for yourself," Lynette said shortly and left. Not so long ago, Debbi would have been so eager to share the details of her experience that she would have tagged along to the barn with Lynette automatically. Not so long ago, she and Debbi had been close.

When Lynette had first come to the ranch in New Mexico, Debbi had said, "It's you and me against the boys." Despite the two years between them, they had been inseparable. "Like sisters," Debbi had said. Because Debbi liked horses, Lynette had forced herself through her fear of them and come out free of clammy hands and quaking guts. In those years, she had been happy. Debbi had almost filled the emptiness left by her mother and Jeremy. To have one person close to her was all Lynette needed. Only Debbi had suddenly stopped liking horses and started liking boys. Overnight, she'd become a woman and discarded Lynette. They still shared a bedroom, but not their deepest feelings any more. Now Debbi sometimes talked to Lynette as if she were a child—"Well, you wouldn't understand. . . . Oh, Lynette, you're such a baby. . . . I can't tell you what he said; you're too young."

After they moved to Lake George, Debbi had found girls like herself. She was never home if she could help it, always off with a pack of teen-agers. She acted as if her family were the managers of a hotel which she lived in temporarily. It hurt whenever Lynette remembered how close she and Debbi had been.

As Lynette finished taking care of Penny, Silver appeared, all lathered up and hanging his head sheepishly. Lynette let him into the paddock, unsaddled him and washed him down, too. Once they had been cooled off, she led the horses to the water trough. They drank as if they'd been out on the desert all day instead of just on a trail for a few hours. Marie, leading a sweat-soaked Gypsy, came into the paddock balancing Gypsy's saddle on her hip.

"Josh shouldn't have let Eddie ride that crazy horse," Lynette said, seeing the way Gypsy rolled her eyes back so the whites showed.

"Nothing crazy about the horse. There was a big burr on her saddle blanket where the saddle rubbed in into her. See?"

"Oh, poor Gypsy," Lynette said looking at the wicked, nutsized stickery thing.

"The boys saddle her?"

38

"Yes. I guess Jeremy doesn't know to check and Eddie's just a little kid. I should have checked myself," Lynette said.

"When a horse acts up, there's usually a good reason," Marie said. "Horses are pretty predictable animals."

"I'm sorry, Marie."

"For what? Nothing to blame yourself for, Lynette. You're always a good kid."

"I am?" Marie had never praised her before.

As if she'd said enough, Marie ducked her head and led Gypsy off to her stall.

Lynette ran back to the house, wondering if Jeremy had made it back yet. A lilt in Debbi's loud laugh told her he probably had. Debbi only laughed that way when she was flirting with a boy. Sure enough, when Lynette walked into the house, she saw Debbi by the fireplace practically nose to nose with Jeremy, who had one hand braced against the stones and a brightness in his eyes that hadn't been there before.

"Hi, Lynette," Debbi said. "Jeremy and me are just getting acquainted. Why didn't you tell me how good-looking he is?"

"Is Eddie all right?" Lynette said.

"Jose says he's O.K. He went up to bed," Jeremy answered her. Then he returned to his conversation with Debbi. "You've really never been to Boston?"

"No, but I was in New York City once. Am I missing much?"

Lynette listened to the easy flow of talk between them. She could have stood and listened to them until the end of the world, and they would never have noticed her there; that was how absorbed they were in each other. Eddie had been competition enough. Debbi would be worse than the girlfriend who had ditched Jeremy. Lynette could say, Debbi, he's mine; you already have a boyfriend, anyway. But even if Debbi took pity on her, it wouldn't do any good. Not when Jeremy seemed so fascinated just looking at Debbi.

"Anybody start supper yet?" Josh asked when he stomped in.

Obediently, Lynette moved into the kitchen area and opened the refrigerator to see what was there to work with.

Chapter 5

Jeremy was sitting on the steps, blocking her passage, when Lynette headed downstairs to the bathroom the next morning.

"Jeremy? Something wrong?" she asked softly and touched him on his shoulder.

"Can't you hear them?" he whispered to her. "They're going at it like a cage full of tigers."

Lynette listened. Josh was roaring at Debbi who was screaming back. "And she's only just gotten home," Lynette said sadly. She didn't have to see them. She knew from experience how they'd look. They'd be standing toe to toe, yelling into each other's red, angry faces.

"They do this pretty regularly?" Jeremy asked.

"They both have tempers."

"Should we intervene? Throw cold water on them?"

"Josh just shouts." Lynette sat down on the step behind Jeremy. What was it this time? Last time the whole battle had been over a soap dish.

". . . a lousy pair of shoes!" Debbi snarled as if in answer to Lynette's question. "I'm fifteen years old. I can't live in *sneakers.*"

"You can live in what I can afford. When you're out there grubbing for a living, you'll see how it is."

"I ain't *never* gonna grub for a living, not like you, too proud to work for someone who's got a head for business. No, not you. You gotta work on a rinky-dink operation that nobody else'd touch with a ten-foot pole."

"Hush up. What kind of girl are you?" Josh said. "You got no respect for your own father. Talk to me like that again, Miss, and I'm telling you, you won't leave your room for a week."

"Who's gonna keep me there? You?"

"You think I can't?"

"Listen, Josh. You can forget I ever asked for that money because you know what I'm gonna do? I'm gonna take a job over to Jay Jay's. He said he'd put me on any time."

"You ain't working for him."

"Then *you* gimme the money for the shoes."

"Here, here, take it all. Take all I got. You're just like your ma. Gimme, gimme, gimme."

"Boy, you got a lot in this wallet, Josh," Debbi said coolly. "A big twenty-dollar bill! Well, I'll see what I can get. Thanks."

Abruptly, the sounds of warfare ceased. Lynette tapped Jeremy on the back. "You can go down now," she said. "It's over."

He gave her a puzzled look. "That quick?"

"Sure." Lynette smiled. She had seen it before. Once Debbi had what she wanted, she relaxed into her usual amiable self, gave Josh a quick kiss and went about her business as if nothing had happened. Josh, though, was probably still standing there with his emotions churning.

Lynette peeked around the stairwell wall to confirm her suspicions while Jeremy slipped into the bathroom. Sure enough, Josh stood alone in the center of the room like a bewildered bear.

"Morning, Uncle Josh," Lynette said, detouring over to give him a kiss of comfort.

"Morning, Lynny," Josh mumbled. He scratched his head and shambled to the front door. "Tell Jeremy to meet me by the fence in the upper field soon as he's done with breakfast."

It was late, Lynette saw now. She and Jeremy had both overslept. Everyone else had already eaten. She cleared the table of dirty dishes that should have been cleared by Debbi. Probably Debbi had run off so fast to catch a ride with Helen, or some other friend, to the shopping center in Glens Falls. Helen liked to go early and have breakfast there and be first into the stores. Lynette had gone with them once. But she couldn't see the fun in trying on clothes she couldn't afford to buy, and she'd made the mistake of saying so. Now Debbi didn't invite her anywhere.

"You cooking breakfast?" Jeremy asked her when he'd come out of the bathroom.

"What would you like?"

"Tell you what," he said. "You do the dishes and I'll make us both some scrambled eggs."

"Good." She dashed for the bathroom and hurried. She wanted to get back to enjoy having Jeremy to herself.

"Jeremy," she said when he was scraping the eggs onto the plates she'd set out. "Are you still glad you came this summer?"

"Sure, I am. It's different from anything I've ever known. Josh is a character. I like him. I like Debbi, too, and Eddie, but I don't think I could take this kind of life for long. Too much hassle over money. You know what I mean?"

Lynette nodded. "That's what Debbi thinks, too."

43

"Yeah, she told me. She wants to be a stewardess so she can travel all over the place." He laughed. "I can just see her giving the pilots heck."

"Debbi's good at looking out for herself."

"Yeah, she's something, isn't she?" He laughed again and set to finishing his breakfast.

Lynette went around arguing with herself all week as she worked on the horses. No sense getting mad at Debbi for being so attractive or at Jeremy for hovering around her. But reasoning it out didn't lessen the pain of seeing Jeremy with Debbi whenever he had free time. Even Eddie complained.

"What's he wanna talk all that dumb stuff with *her* for?" Eddie asked Lynette Tuesday evening after Jeremy and Debbi had stepped outside to look at the stars.

"Why don't you ask him?" Lynette said over the top of the paperback historical romance she had picked up to read.

"How come she's not spending time with her real boyfriend any more? She fight with him again?" Eddie asked.

"She says Bill's mad because she went on vacation with Helen."

"Maybe she'll make up with him soon."

"Maybe," Lynette said.

Wednesday Lynette slogged into the house, soaked from the rain that had been streaming down all morning and smelling rank from the manure she'd shoveled. There stood Jeremy on a chair. He was modeling the flowered skirt Debbi was making for herself. Debbi was sitting on her heels on the floor pinning up the hem.

"Look what she's doing to me," Jeremy complained to Lynette.

"Don't he look cute?" Debbi joked.

"What's the skirt for, a party or something?" Lynette asked. She thought Jeremy looked ridiculous.

"Right. Sara's having a big barbecue Saturday night with dancing, and I'm sick of wearing the same dress to everything. People will think I've only got one."

"You do only have one."

"Yeah, but they don't have to know that. Think this blue will look good on me, Lynette?"

"Sure it will. Everything does."

"Better than it looks on me, anyway," Jeremy said.

"Oh, you!" Debbi tweaked the thick blond hair on his leg.

He yowled and leaped off the chair, reaching for her, but Debbi was already halfway to the bathroom. She slammed the door in his face and locked it, yelling. "Yah, yah, you can't get me."

"Mature, isn't she?" Jeremy said over his shoulder to Lynette.

"You don't look too mature, either," Lynette said, seeing him banging on the door with the skirt still swinging around his knees. He didn't even hear her.

Thursday Lynette scouted the upper fields for the dappled mare. Marie had said the mare got spooked by an airplane, leaped the fence and ran off toward the woods. Lynette found her caught in a blackberry patch and got scratches all over her arms and hands making a passageway out for the horse. Some of the scratches were bloody enough to need tending, so Lynette returned to the house. There she found Jeremy repairing the screen door Eddie had broken. Jeremy didn't even notice her scratches. He was too busy ogling Debbi, who was stretched out in the sunshine on a bath towel wearing a bikini top with her usual jeans.

"Isn't she lazy, Lynette?" Jeremy asked as Lynette waited for him to step aside so she could enter the house.

"I'm not lazy," Debbi said. "I'm working *hard* to get this tan."

"What do you need a tan for? You already look half-baked," Jeremy said.

"Just you wait, Jeremy. When I'm a rich and famous newscaster, I'll never interview you for anything," Debbi said.

"I know you won't. All I'll be is a humble but dedicated teacher improving the minds, hearts and bodies of little kids, just one of the unappreciated builders of a better society, toiling away unsung and—"

"Underpaid," Debbi said.

"Right," Jeremy agreed.

"Maybe I'll interview you for old times' sake, anyway," Debbi said.

They were still involved in their verbal fencing match when Lynette came back out with half a dozen Band-Aids covering the worst of her cuts. Jeremy smiled at her with unseeing eyes. He wasn't making much progress on the door, either. Was it just Debbi's figure that intrigued him so, or did Debbi have some special magic, something Lynette could never hope to grow into? Lynette considered. Debbi was a good-natured person, easy to get along with, but she was a little lazy. If she could get out of working, she did. She could talk a blue streak, but she was only a mediocre student, whereas Lynette wasn't all that good at talking, but she was a hard worker—Josh even said that. And she always had the best marks in her class at school. Jeremy used to be glad she was smart. Now he didn't seem to care about anything she did.

"Jeremy," she complained to him that night, "you never spend any time with me."

"I don't? Who am I with now?" He was lying on a cushion between Eddie and Debbi with the big white cat on his chest watching some stupid game show on television.

"Well, come for a walk with me, then."

"There's no place to walk to, Lynette. It's dark out."

"There's a moon."

"Come on. Sit down and watch television with us."

"Lynny doesn't like television. She thinks it's bor-ing," Debbi said. "All she likes to do is read or cuddle with her horse."

"Lynny's bor-ing." Eddie joined in gleefully to be part of the group.

"Well, there isn't a whole lot to do around here," Jeremy defended her. "I guess reading's as good entertainment as anything."

"You said it! There's nothing to do," Debbi said. "Even if we *do* get to town, all that's there is the hamburger and pizza parlors and the movie."

"Anything good playing at the movie?" Jeremy asked.

"Supposed to be fair. I don't remember the name. I've got that party tomorrow night," Debbi said.

"Well, Lynette, want to go to the movie with me tomorrow night?" Jeremy asked, looking up at her from his prone position.

"Sure, but it's expensive, Jeremy. I don't have enough money."

"She spends every cent she gets on that horse," Debbi said.

"You did, too, when you liked horses," Lynette said quickly.

"I know." Debbi sighed. "Thank heavens I outgrew that."

"Nobody ever takes me to the movie," Eddie said. "Can I go?"

"O.K.," Jeremy said. "I'll treat the both of you if Josh will let us use the truck."

"But Jeremy, you aren't even getting paid this summer. How can you pay for all those tickets?" Lynette said.

"Don't worry about it. I've got plenty saved up from

47

working after school this spring. I'm loaded."

"Hey, big, bold and brawny, lend me some if you're so rich," Debbi said, rolling onto her stomach and beginning to tickle Jeremy.

"Quit that. Hey, quit it, you witch." He started armwrestling with her, but Debbi was strong. He stopped when he saw he wasn't winning. "Woman, you sure know how to take care of yourself," Jeremy said admiringly.

"I'm pretty tough. Have to be in this family. Right, Eddie?"

"Right," Eddie agreed, bright-eyed. "But Lynette's not tough."

"Well, she's tougher than she was when she first joined us. She was such a delicate little thing then. She wilted if you looked at her cross-eyed. Course," Debbi said thoughtfully, "she still hasn't learned how to stick up for herself too good, but she's improved."

Lynette smiled, pleased that they were talking about her. She wasn't sure whether what Debbi was saying was a compliment or not, but she liked the part about being in the family.

"So how about it, Lynette?" Jeremy asked. "Do you like movies?"

"Oh, I love them. I love doing anything with you." She blushed at the gush of her own words.

"Oh, ho, ho, ho!" Debbi said. "Listen at her. She thinks you're a real hero, Jeremy."

"Sure, I'm a hero," Jeremy said. "Show me a damsel in distress and I'll prove it."

"Some hero!" Debbi said. "He's nothing but an overgrown Boy Scout, just a big little boy with a mustache that won't even grow."

Jeremy pulled Debbi's hair and they were back into their mock wrestling match again. Lynette turned her back on them and went to do the dishes, which were still sitting dirty on the table. Josh had gone out with his friends, and Marie had gone back to the barn to see to a horse that was down with the heaves. Just then the blast of a car horn signaled to Debbi that her boyfriend, who had called and made up with her that afternoon, had come for her. She unwound herself from Jeremy and ran off. When Marie came back, Eddie went off to bed. Josh came home shortly after that.

"Hey, Josh," Jeremy said as Josh settled down with a groan on the couch, his arms folded behind his head and his legs stretched out. "O.K. for me to borrow the truck tomorrow night? I want to take the kids to a movie in town."

"Not tomorrow night, Jeremy," Josh said. "Oh, boy, do I ache. Getting old." Marie reached over and massaged the back of his neck. "That's it, honey; that's where it hurts."

"Why not?" Jeremy asked.

"Because I finally got Marie here talked into going to a Grange meeting with me. There's folks there she should know. Never can tell when you're going to need a neighbor. Any other time, you're welcome to use it."

"It's O.K. with me if we skip that Grange meeting," Marie said. "I'd just as soon stay home."

"To work some more? Listen, Marie, life is not just for working. You're supposed to enjoy it, too. Do you good to get away from horses for a change."

"I don't have nothing to say to those people," Marie said.

"Sure you do. Talk about the weather. Talk about our poor dried-up vegetable garden. Talk about anything. They'll listen."

"I'm not much for talking."

"I've noticed," Josh teased.

Marie's face went red.

"Come on to bed," Josh said. "If these young people want to stay up all night, let them. Me, I'm too old." He rose and headed toward his bedroom. Marie followed.

"Sorry," Jeremy said to Lynette. "I thought it might be a good idea if *you* got off the ranch once in a while, too. You work pretty hard yourself, Lynette."

She looked at him with her heart in her eyes. He'd noticed her after all. "We don't have to go to a movie, Jeremy. We can stay home and have fun, anyway."

"We're not going to the movies?" Eddie asked, appearing at the foot of the stairs in the underpants he slept in.

"Why are you up, Eddie?"

"I heard you talking."

"We'll go to the movie some other time. Tomorrow night we'll stay home and play Monopoly together. O.K.?"

"O.K.," Eddie said more agreeably than Lynette expected. "But I was gonna get some popcorn at the movies. I got enough money for that."

"Save your money for next week," Lynette said. "Anyway, if you want, we can make popcorn here."

"Good idea," Jeremy said. "Monopoly and popcorn. Sounds like a fun evening."

In the morning Debbi came down to breakfast with eyes all red and swollen from weeping. "Not again," Josh said.

"Me and Bill broke up last night," Debbi said tragically.

"What's this, the tenth or twentieth time?" Josh asked.

"How can you be so mean, Daddy?"

"Well, I don't see why you get so upset when it happens so often."

"Then you're not going to the party with him tonight?" Jeremy asked. "Good. You can stay home with us. We got a big Monopoly game planned, popcorn and all."

"What are you grinning about?" Debbi asked him. "Think breaking up with your boyfriend's funny?"

The telephone rang and Debbi leaped across the room to answer it. She disappeared around the corner of the fireplace with the receiver. "Don't you grow up to be like your cousin, Lynny. That girl had the makings of a good horse-woman before she turned foolish." Josh sighed." "Well, time to get to work. Coming, Jeremy?"

"I'll be along in a minute." Jeremy waited for Josh to leave, then asked Lynette, "Do you think Debbi's really upset?"

Lynette shrugged. "She told me once that making up with Bill's the best part of their relationship."

"Oh." Jeremy sounded disappointed.

Debbi loped back across the room, already looking more cheerful. "That was Sara. How'd you like to go to that party Bill was going to take me to tonight, Jeremy? Sara says the only reason she didn't invite you was that you'd be the only boy there without a girl, and she thought you'd feel funny. Now that Bill's not coming, you can be my date."

"Oh, yeah? Well, I don't know."

"Please, Jeremy, for me." Debbi put her hands on his shoulders and looked him in the eye. "Sara's one of my best friends. She'll die if I don't come to her party. How's she gonna talk to me about it afterward if I'm not there? You dance, don't you?"

"Sure, I dance."

"I thought so. You move like a good dancer. You're really smooth." Despite the puffiness from her earlier tears, Deb-bi's face shimmered with life. She seemed to give off visible bubbles of vitality.

Lynette quivered, feeling her hold on Jeremy slipping away. His decision didn't surprise her when it came.

"O.K., I'll go," Jeremy said.

Debbi dashed off to call Sara and arrange for someone to give them a ride to the party. Jeremy turned. Seeing Ly-nette, he remembered. "Hey, the Monopoly game! Right? That's what you're looking so glum about?"

She didn't answer.

"Look," he said. "We can play Monopoly any time. I mean if it was the movie, but I'll take you to the movie next week just like I promised."

She turned her back on him and stared at the dishwater instead. It looked murky and foul. She stirred the silverware around in it, trying to control her disappointment. Someday she would be fifteen like Debbi. But probably at fifteen, she'd still be a wisp nobody noticed. No sense thinking about it. Lynette began scrubbing the silverware with the brush. Jeremy wasn't standing behind her any more. She could feel the chill of his absence. She turned around and found he'd gone over to where Debbi was wrapped in a coil of telephone line, talking on the phone again. He was leaning close to Debbi with one hand braced against the fireplace, grinning while he listened to her nonsense.

"Lynette?" Eddie came running into the kitchen area dressed in an inside-out T-shirt and out-at-the-knee jeans. "Can you make me some breakfast?"

"Eat cereal, Eddie. Everybody's done. You slept too late."

"I don't feel like cereal. How come you're not nice to me no more?"

"Because you're not nice to me."

"I ain't done nothing bad to you in weeks," he said indignantly.

She thought about it. He was right. "You eat cereal now," she compromised, "and tonight I'll make you popcorn like I promised."

"When we play Monopoly with Jeremy?"

"He won't be here. He's going to a party with Debbi," she said.

Jeremy left, late, to catch up with Josh and the work on the fences. Debbi sauntered over and said, "You could come to the party too, Lynette, except you're too young."

"I'm only two years younger than you. I'll be thirteen in a couple of weeks."

"Between thirteen and fifteen, two years is a generation," Debbi said loftily and added, "Anyway, somebody has to stay with Eddie."

But why does it have to be me, Lynette thought. She felt blue all day. Even being with Penny didn't cheer her.

Chapter **6**

After Debbi and Jeremy and Josh and Marie had left that night, Eddie nagged Lynette to play a game with him, but she couldn't. It was an effort just to make herself get up and walk from one part of the room to another. For once, she left the dishes in the sink. When Eddie fell asleep in front of the TV, she covered him with a quilt from Josh's room. Josh could carry Eddie up to bed when he got home from the Grange meeting. The house was so empty with everybody gone. She didn't feel like reading.

Restlessly, she stepped outside and looked up at the glossy white moon, which seemed to be resting its weight on the roof of the barn. Insect choruses filled the air with electric static. On an impulse, she ran lightly down the stone steps and across the road to the barn where Penny would be standing asleep in her stall. The horses, penned to be ready for saddling up the next morning for the first trail ride, shuffled and snorted softly in the darkness inside the barn. Lynette slipped into Penny's stall and wrapped her arms around her horse's neck, but her ache didn't ease. Lynette thought of going back to the house, packing her belongings, saddling Penny and riding away on her. They could camp out during the day and ride during the night until they got so far away that no one would know Josh. Then Lynette could get a job as a groom at some stable and pay for her food and Penny's feed by working. Maybe she could ride all the way up to Canada. They would have to get that far away if they didn't want Josh to find them. Of course, it would be hard on Penny. She was on old horse. Suppose no one wanted to take them in? What then? Penny needed the comforts of home. Horses needed caring far more than people, Marie said.

Maybe Lynette ought to just go alone. It would be a lot easier to hide without a horse. Maybe she could find a nice old lady who needed a companion and would be glad of Lynette's young legs and would let her go to school and keep her until Lynette was old enough to take care of herself. Then she would go looking for Jeremy. Probably when she found him, he would be married to Debbi. Debbi and Jeremy would be sitting at the breakfast table in their little house, and Lynette would look through the window and know finally that her secret dream was over, that Jeremy would never be hers.

Lynette kissed Penny good-by. But as she started out of the barn, the urge to do something wild overcame her. Silver was in his stall. Lynette had been afraid of all the big horses years ago. She was still afraid of riding Silver because of his size, but tonight she took a bridle and went recklessly into his stall. He clomped his forefeet and whoofed at her as if to ask what was going on. Standing on tiptoe, she slipped the bridle over his head and got the bit in his mouth and led him out. She opened the gate to the pasture, then stepped on it to help her mount. As if he knew what she wanted, Silver broke into a trot and then a canter as soon as she was astride him. He was no broader than Penny, but Lynette was riding bareback, and in the moonlit pasture everything was exaggerated. She felt as if the pale horse under her with his white mane flying up his neck were part of the moonlight, part of the night, bigger than real and wonderfully mysterious.

Silver cantered easily once around the outside edge of the pasture, slowing at the muddy bottom where the brook came through. It relieved some knot of tension in her to ride around in this scary way. Once more Silver started around the pasture, quickening his speed as he ran. Then instead of making the turn to head up the hill toward the apple tree, he soared over the fence. He took off down the road, his hoofs thumping the asphalt rhythmically as she leaned low over his neck. If a car came, they'd be in trouble. She didn't think she could stop him. The whip of fear chased out her misery. They were part and parcel of the wind. She and the white horse were the wind and this night was a dream happening.

The warm air swished by and the horse clattered on. Afraid that he would never stop, Lynette pulled back on the reins gingerly. To her relief, Silver responded, slowed and turned around at her command.

"That's a good boy," she complimented him. "What a good, good horse you are. And you listen to me, don't you?" To cool him off, she walked him back down the moonlit highway. The world looked strangely simple, just the looming mountain on one side, the empty fields on the other, and overhead an inky, star-stitched sky. If Eddie woke up, he'd be scared finding himself alone. Or suppose the others returned early? They'd wonder where she'd gone. She urged Silver into a trot. He went willingly, eager to get back to his stall. The thrill of overcoming her fear of the big horse and of controlling him percolated through her misery. The summer wasn't over yet and Jeremy was still here, she thought. The wild ride had been good medicine for her.

In the paddock, Lynette dismounted, walked Silver for a while and dried him as well as she could before returning him to his stall. When everything was hung back in place in the barn, and Silver was noisily slurping water from his bucket, she hurried back to the house. Eddie was still asleep. She pulled the quilt he had tossed aside back over him. His face looked so purely beautiful she bent and kissed his cheek. If only he were as sweet awake. She ran up the cavelike staircase that curled around the fireplace.

The aftertaste of the ride came to her—the cool caress of the wind and the rhythmic motion. She had ridden Silver across the pasture and leaped the fence and cantered down the road on him. Wonderful things did happen sometimes.

Past eleven that night, Lynette heard the truck coughing to a stop, then the quiet thud of Josh's boots downstairs, the toilet flushing and silence. Josh and Marie had gone to bed. Jeremy and Debbi got home past midnight. The car which dropped them off had a noisy muffler that announced itself coming and going. Seconds later, they stood in the hall whispering together before they separated. Debbi came immediately to Lynette's bed to see if she was awake. Lynette pretended sleep. She didn't want to hear about the party for which Jeremy had deserted her. If Debbi had been the only one involved, Lynette would have listened gladly. Debbi was a good storyteller. "You'll never guess what happened," she would begin. Then she might say, "And you know what he said to me?" She would quote her own sharp answers to the boy and gleefully relate what had followed. "Aren't I a holy terror?" she'd ask. Lynette would smile and agree, glad to share any part of Debbi's triumphs.

When Debbi was ten and eleven, she used to say, "Boys are so awful." It took Lynette years to understand that despite Debbi's complaints about her brothers and the way they teased and the advantages they had just because they were boys, she enjoyed them. Debbi had grown up with roughhousing. It didn't frighten her the way it frightened Lynette, who had been an only child too long. By the time Lynette had adjusted to the give and take of a big family, everything had changed. The big brothers left home and Debbi discovered boys. Lynette thought discovering boys had made her cousin foolish. All the business about who was interested in whom, and all that talk about what he said and what it really meant and what he really wanted—it was silly.

Lynette heard the squeak of bedsprings as Debbi finally settled down to sleep. Once, after Lynette had stayed awake half the night listening to Debbi talk about a boy whom she didn't even like, Lynette had asked Marie, "Do all girls get silly about boys eventually?"

"I wouldn't know," Marie said.

"Well, how was it when you were a kid?"

Marie had given here a wry look and said, "I don't know, Lynette. My folks believed pleasure was evil so I didn't have friends or get out much."

"Not even to church socials?"

"The church was too far away, the one my daddy believed in. He read the Bible to us himself, and we stayed home and worked the farm."

"But Marie, you must have done *something* that was fun."

Marie smiled. "When I was eighteen and left home, I worked for a fella owned a dude ranch. That was fun. Riding horses."

The hollow sound of Marie's voice as she talked about her childhood made Lynette wonder if some parents could be worse to have than none at all.

In private, Lynette asked Josh, "Were Marie's parents mean?"

"You wouldn't believe how mean," Josh said.

Lynette had shuddered. "But she's happy now?"

"She says she is. I don't know, Lynny. Marie's hard to read. She likes being with the horses, though. I'm sure of that."

Lynette thought Marie liked being with Josh, too. Didn't a smile tease the edges of Marie's thin lips when Josh came into the room? Josh spent a lot of late afternoon hours with his friends and Marie would never go along, but Lynette thought Marie liked being Josh's wife, and that was good. Even though Marie kept a distance around herself that was hard to cross, Lynette liked her and wished her well.

The morning after the party, Lynette woke early despite having slept so little. The only person she met at breakfast was Josh. He was drinking his usual super-sized mug of instant coffee and was sunk back out of sight behind his grizzled whiskers. He looked about as friendly as a hibernating bear.

"Gotta take a day off and go fishing soon if the machinery on this poor excuse for a ranch would just stop breaking down for a minute."

"You going to take Jeremy with you when you go?" she asked.

"Why should I? He's your friend. You entertain him."

She read the tone of his voice and asked, "What are you mad at Jeremy about?"

"I'm not mad at him. He's O.K. Does a good job for a city slicker who don't know nothing and wasn't born with much sense."

"He likes Debbi."

"I see that. Shows how dumb the boy is. You're twice the girl Debbi is, twice as pretty, too."

"Josh!" The extravagant compliment amazed her. "You know I'm not."

"Sure you are. Just you wait. Soon as you hit fifteen,

sixteen, Jeremy's gonna have to stand in line to get a word with you. Trust your old uncle."

Hibernating bear or not, she wrapped her arms around him and hugged him hard. "Thank you, Josh."

"First smile I've seen out of you all summer," Josh said. "You ought to smile more, Lynny."

"I'll try," she promised, and offered to fry a couple of eggs for him.

She felt cheerful enough to ask Jeremy about the party when he joined her in the barn to help her pitch fresh straw into the mucked-out stalls of three horses. Marie wanted these horses kept in because they were lame. Luckily, none was in bad enough shape to need the vet's attentions.

"Did you have a good time last night, Jeremy?" Lynette asked.

"Not too bad. Except they all knew each other. I didn't understand half their jokes. All they talk about is dragracing and hunting.

"Did you dance with Debbi?"

"When I could catch hold of her. She sure doesn't lack for partners."

"Debbi's very popular."

"I'll say."

"I guess you had more fun anyway than if you'd stayed home with Eddie and me and played Monopoly," Lynette said slyly.

His light tone vanished on the instant. "Now, I *told* you I'd make it up to you next week, Lynette," he said. "I know it wasn't nice of me to disappoint you, but you don't have to rub it in."

All she'd wanted was to hear that he was sorry he hadn't stayed home. Instead, she'd managed to annoy him. Debbi would have coaxed him into saying something nice. So much for trying to imitate Debbi. "Anything you do is all right

60

with me, Jeremy," Lynette said anxiously. "All I want is for you to spend some time with me."

"Well, I do." He sounded indignant. "I'm here every day, aren't I?"

"You're here, but not with me."

"I don't know what you want from me, Lynette. Ever since I got here, I feel like you expect more than I know how to give you." His frown struck her like a blow.

"I don't expect anything," she answered quickly. How had this conversation taken such a nasty turn? "It's just you mean more than anybody to me, and I—" She swallowed the rest as his frown deepened.

"You know what's wrong with you?" Jeremy lashed out. "You take everything too seriously. You ought to laugh more and have a good time like Debbi. Then you'd have so many friends, you wouldn't need me at all." He pitchforked half a bale of hay and tossed it into a stall abruptly. She flinched. What had she said to make him so angry at her? He picked up the second forkful and stopped to look at her.

"I'm sorry, Lynette. I didn't mean to yell at you like that. I'm sorry." He didn't sound sorry, just not as angry as he'd been.

A band of sun rays escaped from the cloud cover and glinted off the copper in his hair. His throat rose in a long straight column to his jutting chin. His clear eyes squinted down at her. He looked like her Jeremy, but he wasn't any more. Had he changed because of her? Because she didn't laugh enough? Or had he changed like Debbi, just because he was older? He'd only come this summer because of the breakup with his girlfriend. No sense imagining that he had come to be with her. And he liked Debbi. He liked Debbi better than her. That was how it was. All her dreams of him were fairy tales. He didn't love her. Nobody really loved her.

Chapter 7

Later that morning the lumpy screen of clouds blew away, leaving tissues of white through which the sun blazed brilliantly. Lynette left the apple tree where she had gone to brood and drifted back to the house. She found Debbi baking a cake in the kitchen.

"That stupid Milton," Debbi began as Lynette poked through the refrigerator for something to nibble on. "He opens the oven door right after I tell him not to, and sure enough, the cake falls. I chased Milton and Eddie past the cesspool to that half-dead pine tree. I bet the two of them are still hiding in it."

"I don't see why those boys like to tease so much," Lynette said sympathetically.

"Boys just are that way at a certain age. Course, my oldest brother, Frank—he never was. He was always straight. But Lou and Decker were the worst teases. You remember. Mama used to get them good. She really kept them in line." Debbi stopped stirring the frosting and looked off into some distance inside her head.

"Do you still miss her, Debbi?"

"Mama? Not so much any more. I guess I'm still mad she didn't take me with her. She couldn't of loved me as much as she said to leave me behind with Josh and the boys like that."

"I hope Marie doesn't go away," Lynette said anxiously.

"Marie's a strange one. I don't know about her," Debbi said. "Seems she don't expect a thing out of life except work."

"Josh works hard, too. You don't think *he'll* run away?"

"Josh loves what he does," Debbi said. "Except for not having enough money, he's happy. No matter how bad things get, he's always sure tomorrow will be better."

"I love Josh so much," Lynette said.

It felt good to sit at the kitchen table eating an ear of cold, leftover corn while the sweet scent of the baking cake filled the kitchen and she and Debbi talked as they used to talk to each other about things that really mattered.

"I hope the ranch starts making a lot of money for Josh," Lynette said, holding on to the conversation.

"Not likely Josh'll ever make money," Debbi said. "Best we can hope is he don't get so far behind in the bills that he loses this place. I'd sure hate having to change high schools in midstream."

Let the ranch pay off, Lynette prayed silently. Make Josh come out a winner. Her requests to God were always flung out in desperate moments when she had no one else to turn to.

Later, she went up to her room for a clean T-shirt. As soon as she got near the dresser, she smelled something bad. Nothing looked out of place. She checked the floor and bed and under both beds to see if the cat had done something. Both she and Debbi were neat in the bedroom. They took turns vacuuming and never let dirty clothes accumulate, partly because they didn't have enough extras to allow it. One dresser with two drawers for each of them did for them both.

It was the drawers in the dresser that Lynette now checked. Sure enough, she found the source of the smell. Eddie and Milton! Only they would have left the rotten egg soaking into her good sweater. Josh and Marie had given her that sweater just last Christmas. With an exclamation of disgust, Lynette picked it up in both hands and ran to the bathroom to soak it in the sink. She'd never get that smell out. Even Debbi's cologne wouldn't cover it. It was sickening, horrible.

Cool water didn't take the egg out. She tried hot. Whenever she wore that sweater to school, she felt pretty. Josh said red was her color. Eddie knew how she loved that sweater. How could he have been so mean? She poured in some detergent and left the sweater to soak. Then she ran out to the cesspool where Eddie and Milton had tacked two shaky boards onto the heaviest naked limb of a half-dead tree. The boards made a platform on which they could perch to look out over the road and pastures and barn. The boys weren't there any more. She walked back to the house with anger boiling away inside her.

Debbi was pulling wash out of the machine when Lynette stepped back into the kitchen. "What'd you go tearing out of here in such a hurry for, Lynette?"

"Eddie and Milton dumped a rotten egg on my sweater."

"That'll ruin it for sure. Did you put it to soak?"

Lynette nodded. She threw herself onto the couch. The cat leaped over her head from the couch back where she'd been snoozing and crawled under the TV where she wouldn't be disturbed.

"That little brat," Debbi said, coming to sit beside Lynette on the couch. "You shouldn't let him see how he gets to you. That's why he picks on you so much, you know. If you acted like you didn't care, he'd stop."

Lynette shuddered. It wasn't just Eddie, she wanted to

tell Debbi. It was the weightless feeling of not being loved.

"I'll go see what I can do about your sweater," Debbi said. "Is it soaking in the bathroom? Hey, don't worry, Lynny. I'm good at getting stains out. Didn't I get out most of the paint Josh spilled on the couch? Well, didn't I?"

Debbi was trying to be so kind, but Lynette couldn't respond. She hadn't forgotten that Debbi was one of the misery-makers in her life.

"It's ruined," Debbi came to report later. "Done for. There's a big pink blotch right in the middle of the front. We could try to redye it, maybe."

Lynette shrugged and went to get aspirin for the headache she had developed. Someday she would get a new sweater. What upset her more were the things she was losing that she couldn't replace.

The sound of Jeremy's voice sent her back to the living room in a hurry. There stood Jeremy with Eddie swinging from his shoulder like a monkey hanging on with both hands.

"Why'd you do that to me, Eddie?" Lynette said.

"Do what?" His eyes were wide with innocence. Debbi walked in with the wash basket just then. She went straight to the bathroom and returned with the dripping sweater which she held up as evidence.

"You ruined it good with that rotten egg," Debbi said to her brother.

"I didn't put no rotten egg anywhere."

"Then who did put it in my dresser?" Lynette asked.

"Search me." Eddie shrugged, pretending innocence so successfully that Lynette almost believed him even while she knew he was lying.

"How could you be so mean?" she accused him in a choked voice.

"You was mean to *me* last night," Eddie shot back.

"How?"

" 'Cause you wouldn't play Monopoly or nothing with me."

"Now that's not fair, Eddie," Jeremy said. "I didn't play Monopoly with you, either. You mad at me, too?"

"Uh uh. I'd never put no rotten eggs in *your* room, Jeremy."

"You woudn't, huh. How come?"

" 'Cause I sleep there, too."

Debbi and Jeremy both burst out laughing. Lynette didn't laugh. All she could think of was that Eddie was going to get away with his meanness again.

"All right, Eddie," she said quietly. "From now on, don't you dare ask me to do anything for you. You're a rotten kid, and I'm going to pretend you don't even *exist*."

Whether it was her words, or the cold, final way she said them, Eddie seemed impressed. He stared at her, open mouthed. Then his eyes filled with tears. She didn't care. She never *would* forgive him. She stalked out of the house, heading for the only place where she could find any comfort. Penny should be back from the trail ride by now.

Lynette was filling Penny's oat bucket an hour later when Jeremy found her in the barn. "Lynette," he said. "I want to talk to you."

He leaned his forearms on the half door to Penny's stall. "It's about Eddie. You really do have it in for him, don't you?"

"Shouldn't I? He's rotten to me. He's always doing things to me. Ask Debbi."

"He's just a little kid. He likes to play tricks. There's nothing so bad about him, really. He didn't mean to ruin your sweater. It just happened, and now he's scared you meant what you said to him."

"I did mean it. You and Debbi thought he was so funny.

Well, it was my best sweater he messed up. Everybody lets him get away with murder."

"Come on, don't be that way. Why do you take everything so seriously?"

"I don't know why you don't like me any more, Jeremy. I was always serious. It's not me who's changed. It's you."

"Aw, come on, Lynette. Would I come spend a whole summer here if it wasn't for you?"

"You didn't come for me. I thought you did, but you didn't. You came because you broke up with your girlfriend and didn't have anyplace better to go."

"Hey, that's not a very nice way to put it."

"But it's true, Jeremy. I love you so much, and you don't even like me any more." Her voice teetered on the edge of tears.

"Lynette," he said and stopped. "Listen. . . . You can't need me so much. You're too young. And I'm . . . . You've got to find somebody else to lean on."

He turned and walked out of the barn. Lynette listened to his footsteps retreating and leaned her forehead against Penny's warm, round cheek. The horse snuffled and nipped delicately at her shirt.

"Now I've done it," Lynette whispered. How could she have splattered her feelings all over him like that? She wouldn't be surprised if he never looked at her again.

Chapter 8

Lynette's birthday was a week off, then three days. One morning she woke up and there it was. She was thirteen years old. She sat up in bed, blinking in the sunshine flowing through the window. Thirteen. It didn't feel any different. Debbi was still asleep. Her blond hair was scattered over the pillow, capturing the sunshine. Her face looked younger in sleep without the bold look she wore by day. It seemed to Lynette that Debbi had always been bold and self-assured. No hope then that Lynette would wake up one birthday morning as strong as her cousin.

Judging by the amount of sunlight, it must be pretty late. Lynette wondered why no one had awakened her. Was it because they knew it was her birthday? Last year they hadn't remembered, not until dinner when she'd finally told them, "Today's my birthday," because it was too hurtful to let the day pass without any good wishes at all. Last year they'd pretended they'd known all along and given her her present after dinner. It was a new horse blanket for Penny, which was just what Lynette had wanted. There hadn't been a cake, though, and everyone always got a birthday cake. That was how she knew they really had forgotten. But Debbi had put a candle in a doughnut and lit it for her. The wish Lynette made when she blew out that candle had come true, even if it was just a doughnut. Another summer with Jeremy was what she'd wished for; too bad she hadn't specified what kind.

"You awake?" Debbi asked, opening one sleepy eye.

"Um hum. It's late. I'd better get down to the barn and see if Marie's still saddling the horses."

"Relax. That's all taken care of."

"It is? How do you know?"

"Jeremy helped her."

"Oh."

Debbi stood up and stretched. She looked so good, all parts of her slim and long, plumped out only where they should be. Debbi shucked her pajamas and got dressed. Lynette dawdled. Being thirteen hadn't changed her slender, little girl's body at all. It embarrassed her to look so undeveloped.

"What's wrong?" Debbi asked. "Aren't you coming down for breakfast?"

"You go. I'll be down in a minute."

"Hurry up, then. Maybe you can help me clean the house today."

Lynette nodded. After Debbi strode out, closing the door behind her, Lynette thought, they forgot again. Again, she'd have to remind them. She dressed quickly. Maybe Penny would be off duty today and Lynette could take her for a nice long ride. That would be her birthday treat.

She ran downstairs and into the bathroom without glancing toward the living room, so she didn't see the signs until she'd come out. Then she stopped short and stared.

Strung across the living room were sheets of looseleaf paper with big, bright crayoned letters that spelled out

69

"Happy thirteenth, Lynette." Lynette smiled. Debbi hadn't forgotten. It had to have been Debbi who made the sign because the letters were so neat. The room was empty, but on the long table at the kitchen end were three gift-wrapped boxes. Lynette ran to look. Yes, her name was on them. Yes, they were meant for her, and one was from Jeremy. Tears came to her eyes.

"Surprise!" Debbi leaped through the front door into the living room. Jeremy was right behind her. "Don't touch anything yet," Debbi said. "I have to get everybody. We're having a birthday breakfast for you. Hold on till I get back."

"You're supposed to be happy," Jeremy said. "What are you crying for?"

"Because I'm *so* happy," she said, laughing and crying at once. She heard the clanging cow bell and jumped.

"Debbi's signaling Josh and Marie to come," Jeremy said.

Lynette wiped away her tears and sat down with her hands folded in front of her and a big smile on her face as Josh and Marie trooped in. Eddie was hiding behind Josh who was in stocking feet. He had left his muddy boots just outside the door.

"Happy birthday, honey girl," Josh said, coming to kiss her.

"Thank you, Uncle Josh." She hugged him with enthusiasm and kissed Marie who approached her shyly. Eddie slunk to the end of the table. Lynette had kept her word and ignored him ever since the day he ruined her sweater. Now, seeing him playing with the silverware and sneaking looks at her, she felt inclined to forgive him. Just then Jeremy appeared on the stairs with a hatbox in his arms.

"Ta daa!" Debbi announced loudly. "Here comes the birthday special."

"Guess what's in here, Lynette," Jeremy said.

"A hat?"

"Your birthday cake, as if you didn't know."

"Jeremy and me were up till midnight baking it last night," Debbi said. "I hope the frosting's not runny. The cake was kinda warm when we put it on."

"It's beautiful," Lynette said.

"How do you know? You haven't even opened the box," Jeremy said.

"You and Debbi made it for me, so it's beautiful."

I would've helped, too, but they made me go to bed," Eddie said from just behind her elbow where he had crept to stand.

"You can help me serve it, Eddie," Lynette said. She received the box from Jeremy with ceremony.

"You're not mad at me forever, then?" Eddie asked.

"Not today."

"Happy birthday, Lynny," he said and threw his arms around her waist and hugged her hard.

Lynette assured them that the ripples of frosting dripping down the sides of the high round cake were decorative. Debbi giggled and said, "I told Jeremy it was too warm to frost."

"I didn't have enough room for your whole name," Jeremy explained. "I made the 'happy' too big. Anyway, it tastes good." He scooped some of the excess off the plate and licked it from his finger.

Once they had sung "Happy Birthday," Marie said she had better go. She'd left a girl in charge of the horses and her riders were waiting. "Hope you like the present we got you, Lynette," she said and ran off without even tasting the birthday cake. Lynette cut it. Eddie passed the plates around.

"Open your presents now," Debbi said.

The presents were wrapped in candy-cane paper left over from Christmas, except Jeremy's which was wrapped in newspaper. "We ran out of wrapping paper," Debbi explained. Lynette opened the one from Josh and Marie first. A watch with an expandable band. Lynette said it was wonderful and thanked Josh with a kiss. She had hoped for a new bridle for Penny, but a watch was nice, too. Debbi's gift, which was also supposed to be from Eddie, was a makeup case with eyeshadow, mascara and lipstick in it.

"I thought now you're thirteen, you might want to try some stuff," Debbi said. She usually wore eye makeup when she went out.

Lynette was thrilled, not with the makeup which she never expected to use, but with the idea that Debbi had given her something so grown-up. She hugged Debbi and Eddie both.

"Make me a mustache," Eddie said, picking out the eyeliner pencil and handing it to her.

"I will in a minute, Eddie."

"She still has to open my gift," Jeremy said. "Hey, I hope you like it, Lynette." He was cooking his usual two fried eggs with runny centers which he always sopped up with toast, to Debbi's disgust.

"You saved the best for the last, didn't you?" Debbi asked.

"It's something I made for you. Took me a month," Jeremy said, and again, "I hope you like it."

She opened the box as slowly as she could to savor the joy of opening a present from Jeremy. "A belt!" she exclaimed. "Oh, Jeremy, it's just beautiful." She spread out the hand-tooled leather belt with her name spelled across the back. Running horses were incised at either end of the belt.

"Do you like it?" he asked. "I had to get somebody to draw the horses for me, but I did the tooling myself."

"I love it. I'll keep it forever." She half rose, wanting to hug him as she had the others, then sat back down shyly.

"Don't I get a kiss, too?" he said, holding his arms out to her.

72

Bidden, she ran to hug and kiss him. He hugged her back, but released her abruptly as if he were suddenly embarrassed to be kissed by her.

Josh wondered aloud if he could have seconds on the birthday cake.

"You're getting a paunch on your paunch, Papa," Debbi said, "Save the rest for supper."

Josh patted the belly spilling over his belt. "This here is all muscle, Debbi. What to you mean, paunch? Do I have a paunch, Lynny?"

"You look fine to me, Uncle Josh."

He patted his belly absently and reflected, "I guess I'm not as pretty as I used to be. Guess a man my age don't need to be specially good looking." But when Lynette cut the second piece and put it down in front of him, he said, "Save it for later, honey. I'd best get back to the salt mines, or the show ring, as the case may be. Jeremy, you want to take the kids swimming this afternoon after the chores are done? You can borrow the truck."

The chorus of thanks followed him out the door.

It rained that afternoon, but Lynette, with Eddie's support, begged to go down to the lake anyway, since they didn't often have transportation and a chance for all of them to go together. Finally, Jeremy said, "Oh, what the heck, why not? It's not raining that hard."

Just as they drove onto the broken asphalt of the parking area, the sun came out and the rain stopped.

"There," Lynette said, "Even the sun knows it's my birthday." They all agreed that must be so.

Jeremy raced her over the grassy level to the lip of sandy beach laid in by the state for public use. He dove into the water first, but he praised her for jumping in right after him without hesitating at the chilly water. The lake was so deep, it never did warm up much. They swam out to the float, Lynette and Jeremy and Debbi. Debbi swam awkwardly with her head high out of the water. Lynette did a proper crawl stroke. While Debbi sunbathed on the float, Jeremy swam off to investigate the cup-shaped rock on the tiny island a hundred feet off shore. Lynette went back to where Eddie was paddling around alone in the shallows and offered to play tag with him in the water. It was a perfect afternoon.

That evening, Jeremy said to Lynette approvingly, "You've had a smile on your face all day."

"It was such a wonderful, wonderful birthday," she said. "I love the belt, Jeremy. I guess you do think of me sometimes when I'm not with you."

"Hey," he said. "You know I'd never forget you." He pinched her cheek and chucked her under the chin as if she were a little kid.

"Remember that I'm thirteen now," she reminded him. "I'm only four years younger than you are."

"Only! Boy, you're funny," he said.

She went down to the barn to take care of Penny, who'd been out on the trails twice that day with little kids who needed a small gentle animal. Jeremy still considered her a child, Lynette thought. That was the relationship he was used to, big brother to helpless little girl. Well, she'd just have to grow up faster so that he'd begin to treat her the way he treated Debbi. Still, it had been such a lovely day. She was so happy that she sang under her breath as she groomed Penny and then went to help Marie with the other horses. Time enough remained in the summer for all kinds of good things to happen.

Chapter 9

Right after Lynette's birthday, Jeremy got involved with a project that took all his free time. He was building a fort with Eddie, and sometimes with Eddie and Milton. The fort was supposed to be a secret place. Eddie and Jeremy discussed it in numerous hushed conferences which halted whenever anyone got close enough to overhear them. Since they were hammering away in a clearing a few feet off one of the main trails and had only thinly disguised the area with loose branches of juniper across the opening, everybody knew their secret place.

As the last precious days of the summer slipped by, Lynette grew impatient. One morning she suggested a berry-picking expedition to Jeremy and he refused to go. He said he had to work on the fort.

"Why does he want to play games with Eddie all the time? He's too old for little kids' games," she complained to Debbi as they loaded the washing machine.

"He likes little kids," Debbi said. "Didn't he tell you? He's gonna be a teacher or a recreation director or something like that."

"Jeremy never tells me anything," Lynette said. "He's too busy to talk to me."

"Oh, fiddlesticks," Debbi said. Fiddlesticks was the word she'd substituted for the one Josh had said he didn't like to hear a girl using. "He'd spend more time with you if you weren't always begging for his attention."

"Debbi!"

"Well, I'm sorry, but someone has to give it to you straight. Nobody likes someone after them all the time. Remember how mad I got at that guy who was always hanging around me last year? He stared at me with those big moon eyes till I thought I'd go crazy."

Lynette considered. "I don't beg Jeremy for anything. I just ask."

"But you *look* at him. You look at him like he's God or something."

Lynette blushed. Did she look at him with her heart in her eyes? "I can't help it, Debbi. Tell me what I should do, then."

"Just cool it. Give him some room."

Lynette wrung her hands. "I'll try," she said. But with time getting short, it was hard to be cool.

Twice that week she offered to help them build the fort. It was a way to be near Jeremy, but Eddie had turned anti-female now that Jeremy was here.

"No girls building *my* fort," Eddie said. "Think I want it to fall down?"

"I can swing a hammer just as well as you," Lynette told him.

"No, you can't. Jeremy taught me to hammer straight. Anyways, our fort is for guys only. Right, Jer?"

Jeremy was knocking mud from his work boots before going into the house. "No self-respecting girl would want anything to do with that fort, Eddie," he said.

"So there!" Eddie said to Lynette, believing Jeremy had agreed with him.

The fort kept Jeremy away from her during the daytime hours, and Lynette blamed the teen coffee house in the village for his absence at night. She was excluded from the coffee house because she didn't have a high-school identification card yet. In the fall, when she entered high school, she would receive a card. For now, she had to watch Jeremy and Debbi dashing off together when one of Debbi's friends honked to let her know they were waiting in the road below the steps. Debbi had wangled a card for Jeremy from a girl whose brother never used it.

"What's so great about that coffee house, anyway?" Lynette asked one Friday night when Debbi asked her to do the dishes so Jeremy and Debbi could take off early. "You don't even like coffee, and you never used to go."

"Yeah, but now everybody's started going. There's a new guy who plays a guitar. . . . But you're not missing much, Lynette. All we do is sit around and talk and maybe dance a little if the turntable isn't broken and somebody remembers to bring records. Its' really bor-ing."

"If it's so boring, why do you and Jeremy keep going?"

"Listen," Debbi said, switching tactics, "next summer you'll be old enough to come, too."

Lynette bit her lip. Next summer Jeremy wouldn't be here. She wouldn't want to go then. It was now that she longed to go with them so she could squirrel away memories of being with him to keep her through the winter.

Through all her frustrations, Lynette hadn't let herself become really jealous of Debbi. It wasn't Debbi's fault she was so appealing to boys. Besides, Debbi still had her steady boyfriend, Bill, who came first—when she wasn't mad at him. But the night of the rodeo, Lynette's defenses broke down.

Josh and Marie were treating the whole family to the rodeo, Jeremy too, even though the six tickets cost more than they could properly afford. "What's money for, anyhow?" Josh said. He had sold a horse that day, a palomino with which Marie had done wonders. It had brought a good price. Never mind the unpaid bills. Tonight they would celebrate. Lynette, Eddie, Debbi and Jeremy rode in the open back of the pickup truck.

Lynette was excited. "I like rodeos," she said.

"You've only been to one," Debbi pointed out. She was sitting with her back against the side of the truck. Jeremy dropped an arm casually around her shoulder. Debbi didn't lift it up and ask with disgust, "What's this thing doing on me?" She'd done that once to a boy she didn't like too well. Instead, to Lynette's surprise, Debbi acted as if she was used to having Jeremy's arm around her.

"I ain't been to no rodeos never," Eddie said. He was the most excited of them all.

"I know two of the guys in the roping and tying contest," Debbi said. "Saw one of them break his arm on a bucking bronco last time I went."

"I bet none of these cowboys have ever been further west than the western border of New York," Jeremy said.

"They're good, though," Debbi assured him while he played with a lock of her hair, twisting it around his finger and letting it spring loose. Lynette watched, not liking what she saw.

At the rodeo, they all stood at the railing that ran around the field where the main events took place. All of a sudden, Jeremy lifted Debbi up onto the rail so she could see the opening parade better. Debbi was five foot nine and no lightweight. Lynette was shocked. The image of Jeremy lifting Debbi and then standing beside her with an arm around her waist to steady her—until an official came and

78

said she had to get off the rail—blotted everything else out for Lynette. She didn't see the calf-roping or the fancy rope-twirling or the bucking horses kicking up their heels as they exploded from the chutes. All she saw was that grin on Jeremy's face when he lifted Debbi.

Later that night when they were alone in the bedroom, Lynette asked, "Do you like Jeremy an awful lot, Debbi?"

"He's all right," Debbi said casually. "At least he doesn't act like he owns me the way Bill does."

"But don't you love Bill?"

"Oh, Bill! He can be so bor-ing," Debbi said. "Hey, you're not jealous, are you? You love Jeremy like a brother, don't you? I mean, it's not like you'd feel about a boyfriend, is it?"

"I love Jeremy," Lynette said sadly. "I don't know just how."

"Well, anyway, in two weeks the summer will be over, and he'll be all yours again." Debbi yawned. "I'm no good at long-distance relationships." She went to sleep then. Nothing bothered Debbi. Even times after she broke up with Bill, she'd fall asleep as soon as she put her head down on the pillow.

Lynette lay awake, smoldering with jealousy. Finally, when she was sure everyone was asleep, she got up, dressed and ran down to the barn. Penny was tired from a long day of trail rides, but Lynette coaxed her out of her stall. "You won't mind a little walk with me, Penny," Lynette told the horse, who followed her obediently into the paddock and through the gate into the pasture. Lynette walked beside Penny's head, holding the halter as if she were holding hands with a friend. Penny's soft whoofs of breath sounded like sympathetic responses as Lynette told her, "Jeremy's in love with Debbi." Saying the words was like closing her hands on a thistle. The sting of the words made them true.

She reached the smooth bench of rock which glowed from

reflected moonlight and sat down. Penny bent her head to graze on the long grass at the edges of the rock outcropping. Sitting there, Lynette was facing the house. It looked like a shadow against the even darker mountain on which it nested. Lynette shivered as a bat swooped by and veered off toward the barn. Penny's presence kept her from being afraid in the darkness where the nocturnal animals were prowling for food—raccoons and mice and owls and bats. Penny was the only creature she had left now that Jeremy wasn't hers any more. But it wasn't fair. She had loved Jeremy for so long. She needed him so much. Why couldn't he love her a little when she loved him so much? It seemed the very strength of her feeling should draw him to her, but it wasn't working out that way.

She knew what she should do. She should resign herself to losing him to Debbi and be glad for him, but it was hard. Even though Debbi was her cousin, and even though she liked and admired Debbi, still a stubborn voice inside Lynette said, "He's mine."

The cicadas' harsh chorus went on and on below the shushing of the wind. Penny's hooves clicked against stones as she ambled down toward the brook. A gauze scarf surrounded the moon. Stars were lost behind the passing clouds. Despite the breeze, the mosquitoes located Lynette. No point sitting there to provide a meal for them. No point waiting for the lump expanding in her chest to stop suffocating her, either. She tracked Penny down to the brook and led her back to the barn.

Chapter 10

A night's sleep and the bright light of morning was all Lynette needed to start hoping again. When she found out Debbi planned to go to West Point with Bill for the whole next day, Lynette thought of a way to get Jeremy to herself. He had been intrigued by the Indian arrowhead Marie had found on one of her trail rides. He might be interested in picnicking at the spot to look for an arrowhead himself. It would be fun to help him find one. Of course, Eddie would want to come along, but she could remind Jeremy of the trouble Eddie had been on their last excursion. Not that the burr under Gypsy's blanket had been Eddie's fault. Nine-year-olds couldn't be held responsible for things like that. Well, if Eddie ended up coming with them, O.K. The thing to do was get Jeremy interested, and even before that, she'd better see if Marie could spare the horses.

Late that afternoon, after the trail riders had all gotten into the cars that lined the barn side of the road and departed, Lynette ran down to help Marie with the horses. The barn was encased in amber light which paled as it rose to the top of the sky. From their nests under the eaves, barn swallows looped through the varnished air and dipped low over the heads of the horses patiently waiting to be unsaddled.

Penny greeted Lynette with a whinny. Her ears were perked forward, but her head hung wearily. "Is Penny all right?" Lynette asked Marie in alarm.

"Think so, but I'm gonna give her a few days off," Marie said. "She can rest up in the pasture."

"Then I shouldn't ride her?"

"Oh, an easy ride with you isn't gonna hurt her any, Lynette."

"I was thinking of taking Jeremy up to where you found those arrowheads—thinking of going tomorrow, if that's O.K."

"Sure," Marie said. "I'll draw you a map tonight after supper."

Lynette removed Penny's tack and hung it in its place in the barn. Once she'd been cooled down, Penny nudged her way into the crowd of horses at the water trough and took a long, noisy drink. Next, Lynette unsaddled the sturdy, round-bellied Morgan with the white blaze that was Marie's favorite. By the time Lynette had taken care of four horses, Marie had finished the other nine and was examining Penny's feet.

"Did she pick up a stone or something?" Lynette asked.

"No, she's just gettin old, so her muscles ache and her feet are tender." Marie patted Penny's haunch and began to massage the horse's legs.

"Old," Lynette repeated. A shiver went through her. "Marie, if Penny got too old to use on the trail, would anything—would you have to get rid of her?"

"It don't pay to worry about things before they happen," Marie said gently.

"I *can't* lose Penny."

"Penny's got some good years in her yet," Marie said. "She's not more than twenty, twenty-two. When I was a kid, there was a horse I liked still going strong at twenty-six. Big headed, plug-ugly stallion, but he tried to talk to me like Penny does with you. He'd follow me around like a pet dog if he was free, and he'd lean his big, ugly head on my shoulder." She smiled to herself, then asked, "Where is Josh, anyways?"

"He said he needed a recreational break," Lynette said. Recreational break was Josh's way of saying he was going out with his cronies. Josh said a man had to have his hobbies, and his included being with his friends, hunting in the fall and buying horses and saddles he didn't need. Marie had no hobbies, but she didn't seem to begrudge Josh his.

"You never complain about anything, do you, Marie?" Lynette said with admiration.

"I've got a good life, nothing to complain about," Marie said.

"A good life?"

"Sure. I've got Josh and the horses and enough to keep me busy. That's a whole lot more than I ever thought I'd get."

Lynette thought about that. It seemed to her that Marie was easily satisfied. It would be good to be that way instead of going around hungry for what she didn't have all the time. Of course, Marie did have both Josh and the horses. All Lynette had was Penny, who was growing old and who, as much as Lynette loved her, was not a person.

Lynette stayed until every horse had been fed and either set loose in the pasture or closed into a stall for the night. Then she climbed the steps to the house right at Marie's heels. Josh's voice was going like a carnival ride inside the house.

"He sounds mad," Lynette whispered.

"I don't think so," Marie said, but they entered cautiously.

"You got enough nails off me to build a whole army base, let alone one puny little fort," Josh bellowed at Eddie and Jeremy. They were sprawled on the couch together facing the TV which was on, but not loud enough to compete with Josh.

"We need lots of nails," Eddie said. "Our fort's gotta be strong enough to hold off an emeny attack." Eddie never could say "enemy" correctly.

"Any enemy attacks on that trail are likely to be from me if I find my nail can empty again," Josh said. "I mean it, you kids. I'm gonna have your hides if you don't leave my stuff alone. And where was you, Jeremy, when I was calling for you all over creation this afternoon? Think the fort's more important than shoring up that corner of the barn that's fixing to cave in?"

"I'm sorry, Josh. I didn't hear you. We were up at the fort, and I thought you'd gone to town. I looked for you before Eddie and I left."

"Yeah, well, just you keep in mind who pays your salary hereabouts."

"What salary is that, Josh?" Jeremy asked.

"Well, now, there ain't none; that's true. Unfortunate, but true." Josh looked stumped for the minute. "Anyway," he continued more calmly, "stop taking the nails. The old wood in that back shed was one thing, not much use for that, but the nails come out of expenses that we got altogether too much of as is."

"Jeremy and Milton and me are gonna have a war," Eddie said, veering away from the subject of nails.

"A war?" Josh repeated. "What do you need to make a war for? We got plenty going on in the world already."

"Yeah," Eddie agreed. "We're gonna have a real war with bombs and spies and road blocks just like on TV."

"That so? And when's your war coming off?"

"Soon as Milton can stay over. We're gonna bivo—biva— What's that word, Jeremy?"

"Bivouac. It's O.K., isn't it, Josh, if the kids and I camp out some night up there at the fort?"

"You gonna make a fire?"

"Probably."

"Dangerous in these woods, especially now. We had a dry summer."

"I know all about campfires, Josh. I'm not an Eagle Scout for nothing," Jeremy said.

"Yeah. Well, O.K." Josh rubbed his hand over his beard. "We gonna eat tonight? That Debbi! Some housekeeper she is. She ain't ever around when we need her."

"Debbi went sailing with Bill," Lynette said. "She told me to tell you."

"Debbi back to seeing that boyfriend of hers again? I thought she was done with him," Josh said.

Lynette looked at Jeremy who had no doubt thought the same thing. She understood the pained look on Jeremy's face well. She could have warned him that Debbi was always picking up, trying out and discarding boys. Debbi treated boys the same as clothing. She got tired of things long before they wore out and wouldn't wear them again even if she had nothing with which to replace them. Lynette wasn't about to tell things like that about her cousin, though, not even to Jeremy.

"Would you like to go looking for arrowheads with me tomorrow afternoon, Jeremy?" she asked in a rush. "I could show you where Marie found hers and we could have a picnic."

"That'd be nice," he said. "But when Josh finishes working me to death, I've got to work on that fort. Only two weeks left before I leave."

85

"This summer did go by fast," Jeremy said, turning away from Lynette's distress to look at the TV.

"How about if I come up and help you with the fort, then?" Lynette said, her eyes still on Jeremy.

"It's an army fort just for guys." Eddie raised himself up on his elbows to answer her question. "Isn't it, Jeremy?"

"Girls join the army, too," Lynette said.

"Not this army. Nobody's allowed but me and Jeremy and Milton," Eddie said. "You got to know the secret password to get in. Right, Jeremy?"

"Right, tiger." Jeremy kept his eyes fixed on the TV screen.

"Seems to me it was Lynette Jeremy came to see this summer, not you, Eddie-big-britches," Josh said in his old amiable voice. His anger about the nails was long gone.

Lynette looked at Josh gratefully. "Jeremy?" she asked.

"Hey," he said, "It's Eddie's fort."

Josh grunted and marched to the refrigerator. "What've we got to eat in this place? Ain't nobody hungry but me?"

Marie came out of the bathroom saying, "I'll cook us up some spaghetti, Josh."

Lynette was silent all the while she helped Marie get dinner. During the meal, Josh and Jeremy argued about something. Lynette heard their voices at a distance. He doesn't like me any more, she thought. It wasn't just Debbi who was keeping him away. Debbi was no longer available to him, and still he found excuses not to spend time with Lynette. Eddie's fort! If Jeremy liked her at all, he'd want to spend some of the last few days with her.

Had she changed so much for the worse since she was a little girl of eight? Then he used to tell her how smart and pretty and capable she was. Something had to be wrong with her now that Jeremy didn't even want to be near her. Did he find her boring because she was so involved with

86

Penny? She didn't read as much as she used to. Maybe she should talk to him about books. She didn't laugh and tease and joke around the way Eddie and Debbi did. That could be it. They were just more fun to be with than she was. It was bad, too, that sometimes she stepped on people's feelings when she was careless, and it was true she was jealous of all the attention he paid to others. No doubt Jeremy thought she was mean to Eddie. All in all, now she was being honest with herself, she could see that she mustn't be too appealing to him. It depressed her to discover that she didn't even deserve to be loved.

She was so down that she barely noticed the hug Josh gave her when she said good-night later. Josh's affectionate gestures were awkward and infrequent and therefore to be treasured, but she had never felt so poor as when she went off to bed that evening.

Chapter 11

Lynette caught the last blush of dawn through her bedroom window. No one else was awake. Quietly she padded downstairs. She hoped that the flushing of the toilet and water trickling down the pipes in the sink wouldn't waken Josh or Marie. Outside, the dew-wet world was alive with singing birds as she ran to the barn. It was so beautiful with the pink sky and the music. Let Jeremy go to work on Eddie's stupid fort. Let Debbi, who had gotten in late last night after her day at West Point, sleep all day. Lynette had plenty to keep her busy.

First, she mucked out Penny's stall, after releasing Penny to the pasture to begin enjoying her second day off. They would go for a leisurely ride together later. Next, Lynette took down all the grubby-looking tack, got the neat's-foot oil and rags and climbed up the stepped bales of straw to sit and work hidden away next to the window. She cleaned the cobwebs from the fly-specked window so should could look out and watch Penny in the pasture. Debbi poked her head in the doorway, her blond hair hanging down like a cascade of sunshine. "Lynette, where are you?" Debbi yelled. She waited a minute, then left.

Rubbing oil into the tack made Lynette feel better. Marie

was right. Work was good for you. When Marie came to get ready for her morning riders, Lynette climbed silently down to help her saddle up the horses.

"Don't worry about the stalls," Lynette said. "I'll muck them all out this morning."

"Don't know what I'd do without your help, Lynette. I really do appreciate it."

"Thanks, Marie."

"Can I say something personal to you?"

"Sure." Lynette was surprised. Marie had never offered a personal comment before.

"That Jeremy," Marie began, "he's just a boy. You scare him away when you let him see how bad you want him. . . . At least, that's how I see it. . . . I could be wrong. . . . You think about it."

Lynette swallowed. Even Marie had noticed how Jeremy avoided her. Then it wasn't Lynette's imagination. She waited to hear more, but Marie had had her say and was going about her business. Lynette watched her. The pouches under Marie's eyes and her plain, long-jawed face made her look older than her thirty-two years, but Lynette no longer considered Marie homely. Instead, she saw her sweetness. Marie was a kind person. Look at the ways she had reached out of her shyness to try and tell Lynette something. What was it Marie had said?

When the stalls were clean, the sun was at full strength in the paddock. Lynette had pitched fresh hay under each feed bucket for the horses that would stay overnight in the barn. She finished oiling the tack, then went up to the house to see about lunch. Debbi was vacuuming the living room.

"You missed going swimming this morning," Debbi said. "Friend of mine came by. Eddie went with me. I looked for you but couldn't find you nowhere."

"I was in the barn. Where's Jeremy?"

"He worked with Josh this morning cutting wood. Now he's up at that stupid fort with Eddie and Milton-the-goon. Yuk. I hate that kid."

"Debbi? How come you decided you like Bill better than Jeremy?"

"Well, for one thing, Jeremy's leaving soon, and I told you I'm not much for long-distance relationships. I hate writing letters. For another, Bill's more my type."

Lynette sat down, drawing her knees up under her chin. She might learn something from this. "Why's Jeremy not your type?" she asked.

"Oh, you know. I'm tough, like Bill. I like to kid around and fight and lace into a guy. Jeremy's so tender-hearted."

"He talks to you a lot," Lynette said wistfully.

"Well, that's 'cause I'm more his age than you are. Listen, Lynette, I got to tell you something. Boys don't like it when you chase after them with your heart in your hands. Nobody wants anybody lying at their feet so they can't move without kicking you."

Lynette realized she'd now heard the same thing twice in one morning from two very different people. "I don't know," she said. "I just know he cared about me a whole lot once, but he doesn't any more."

"Well, don't take it so hard. In a few years you'll have more boys falling all over you than you'll know what to do with, and Jeremy won't mean beans to you."

"I think I'll take Penny for a ride now," Lynette said. Debbi didn't know what she was talking about if she thought Jeremy would ever not matter.

"Listen," Debbi said. "Bill's taking me to the movie in town tonight. You can come, too, if you want."

"No thanks." She didn't need charity. "I'll be fine. You go and have fun."

Lynette saddled Penny with the lightest-weight English

saddle in the barn and was mounted before she remembered she'd forgotten to eat lunch. She'd just do without for another few hours.

The day continued to be glorious. The clouds were high-flying streamers against a polished blue sky. Plenty of cool breeze to temper the sun. The trees gossiped busily with one another, swishing and shuffling and sighing as if every leaf had something special to say.

"Let's ride the easy path through the spruce woods and maybe we'll see how the fort's coming, Penny," Lynette said. She wasn't going to hang around Jeremy, just ride by and glance his way.

Penny's day and a half of idleness had freshened her. She even seemed eager to run. Lynette held her in, taking pleasure in the creak of the saddle and the gentle rocking motion as Penny walked. They entered the shaded tunnel of the bridle path where it was cool and damp and the air was like green licorice. There Lynette let Penny trot on the needle-cushioned path. A chipmunk skittered across and ran halfway up a tree trunk before it stopped to check on them. On her own, Penny moved into a slow, easy canter. Lynette let her go. Some days Penny forgot how old she was and acted frisky as a young mare. This was one of those days. The path continued through a mixed woods of ash and birch and hickory. The airy pattern of leaves was pierced by broad shards of sunlight. Someone shouted, but Lynette couldn't make out the words. Then she heard Milton's voice yelling, "Halt, or we'll shoot."

Lynette leaned back in the saddle as she began to rein Penny in.

"Halt, I told ya," Milton shouted. He popped out of the bushes alongside the path, startling Penny who jerked forward to run away.

"You idiot!" Lynette yelled at Milton. She didn't *see* Eddie at all, but a hard object the size of a baseball dropped from overhead and exploded in a geyser of water at Penny's feet. Penny reared and came down neighing in fear. Then she took off at a run. Lynette leaned low over the horse's neck, trying to calm her.

"It's all right, Penny. Nothing happened. Whoa, now. Take it easy. Whoa, you'll hurt yourself running when you're supposed to be resting."

Penny was halfway back to the paddock, having covered the complete loop into the spruce-guarded passage, before she began walking again. Her sides heaved and Lynette grieved over her until they were back at the barn. Then Lynette dismounted. She cradled Penny's beautiful head in her hands to comfort her. "Poor baby. You got so scared. That rotten little monster and his friend. This time they're not going to get away with it."

Lynette burned with rage. She cooled Penny down and dried her off before putting her back into the stall to rest. There, the explosion resounded again in Lynette's mind. What had it been that dropped from overhead and splashed at Penny's feet? Sudden fear made Lynette lift each of Penny's hoofs in turn and examine them. The first two were all right. The rear left hoof had a small triangular piece of glass embedded in it. Lynette pried it out with the hoof pick in her jeans pocket and ran to the first-aid box for the iodine. She poured some into the puncture to keep Penny from getting infected. Lynette didn't see any more glass, but on the left front foot she saw blood.

"I'll kill him," she said, feeling anger and rage. She ran outside for help. Marie, who knew horses best, was out on the trails. Josh then. But where would he be? Running across the road without looking, Lynette nearly got hit by a speeding logging truck. Jeremy was walking down the steps to the road.

"What happened?" he asked. "Are you all right?" He sounded really worried.

"I'm O.K., but Penny's hurt. Where's Josh? He's got to look at Penny's foot."

"I think he went down by the lake. I'll get him for you."

"Jeremy"—she stopped him—"why did you let Eddie throw glass on a bridle path? Don't you know horses' hoofs are sensitive?"

"I wasn't even there. I'd gone down to the house to get stones for the fireplace we're building. When I got back, Eddie said—Lynette, it was an accident."

"No, it was *not*. He threw a jar full of water at Penny and me."

"It was accidental, though. You should have seen him. He was white as a sheet. He says the jar slipped out of his hands."

"Nothing slipped. He threw it. He always lies. Do you think he's going to admit something that would get him in trouble? And even if all he did was throw the water, that's dangerous, too. You can kill someone by making a horse rear like that." She shuddered. "Why am I standing here arguing with you? I have to get help for Penny."

"You stay with your horse. I'll call him." Jeremy sprinted back upstairs to the house while Lynette returned to Penny's stall. Penny was standing inside with her head hanging forlornly, water dripping from her nose and the bucket empty. Lynette refilled it. Then she began cleaning Penny's hoofs with the hoof pick. The sensitive frog at the back of the hoof was still bleeding. She knew that a horse could get infected and go lame from even a minor wound, and an old horse like Penny didn't heal so quickly. A sense of doom seized Lynette as she thought of Penny permanently lamed.

"Oh, Penny," Lynette mourned, pressing herself against her horse's copper hide.

Penny shook her mane and shifted restlessly from foot to foot. She seemed to be suffering. To make her more comfortable, Lynette threw down more straw on the floor of her stall. She filled the feed bucket with the precious sweet feed that Marie kept for horses who weren't eating right. Finally, Josh lumbered in. His grizzled face was a welcome sight to Lynette.

"Had a little accident?" Josh asked, stopping beside Penny's head and giving Lynette a pat on the back. Anxiously, she watched him handle Penny. Josh lifted one foot at a time with care and studied each.

"Need better light. Let's take her outside," he said.

"She had a piece of glass in her rear left hoof," Lynette said, "and the front left one is bleeding at the frog."

Josh positioned Penny just outside the barn door. He picked up the bleeding hoof. Penny tried to pull her foot out of Josh's probing fingers, even ducking her head back with her mouth open as if she'd like to bite him.

"Hold her head, Lynny," Josh said. Lynette moved to do just that. "Doesn't look too bad here," he rumbled. "We'll put some disinfectant on it, but it looks O.K., I'd say. We'll get Marie to look at it when she gets back this afternoon." He went for the first-aid kit and poured some more iodine on both hoofs. "Well, old girl," he told Penny. "I'd say you'll be fit as a fiddle in the morning."

"What about Eddie?" Lynette said.

"You want me to give him a whack? Jeremy says it was an accident."

"Jeremy wasn't there, and throwing water on a horse is dangerous, too, even if that's all Eddie did."

Josh nodded. "You've got a point there. He sure don't use good sense. Course he's only a little feller. Well, I'll have a talk with him."

Lynette flushed with anger. A talk! Was that all? Just

94

because he was the baby, Josh spoiled him. The only one who ever punished Eddie for anything he did wrong was Debbi. Maybe Debbi would do something about this, and if she wouldn't, well, then, Lynette was going to have to take care of it herself. She couldn't let him get away with hurting Penny. She'd teach him a lesson no matter what Jeremy thought.

Chapter **12**

Nursing her anger, Lynette avoided Jeremy all the rest of that afternoon. She wanted Eddie's punishment to fit the crime.

She was peeling potatoes for dinner when Eddie charged into the house, chasing the cat who had a mouthful of feathers.

"You sneak-thief-murderer you!" Eddie was yelling. The cat squeezed behind the refrigerator. Eddie got a poker from the fireplace.

"Put that down," Lynette ordered. "You leave that cat alone."

"He went at the nest in the climbing tree and ate another baby bird."

"He's a hunter," Lynette said.

"I'm gonna fix him so he don't hunt no more baby birds."

"You are not. *You're* the one needs to be taught a lesson," she said. "You dropped that glass jar in front of my horse. That was a *horrible* thing to do."

"I didn't do it. Leastways, I didn't mean to," Eddie squealed.

"Liar."

"Am not."

"You're bad, Eddie. You're a mean little kid."

96

"Am not." He sounded close to tears. When his eyes filled, he turned his back on her so she couldn't see him and went to switch the television on, forgetting the cat. He plunked himself down on the cushions on the floor and sat with his fists under his chin and his elbows on his knees. Lynette seethed. He hadn't even said he was sorry.

Luckily, the barbecue sauce she had concocted for the franks began erupting in violent splats. Lynette turned her attention to the sauce. Just then, Debbi came downstairs all dressed up for a date, wearing blue eye shadow and finger-length false eyelashes.

"Debbie, I want to talk to you about Eddie," Lynette said. She set the heat lower on the stove.

"Look at what Bill gave me." Debbi waved her arm at Lynette. "It just came in today. He ordered it at the jewelers before we had our fight last month. Isn't it something?"

Lynette didn't see anything but Debbi's waving arm. "Debbi, Eddie needs to be punished. He threw a jar of water at Penny and me on the trail today."

"Will you *look*," Debbi flapped her wrist harder under Lynette's nose.

"It's an I.D. bracelet. That's nice."

"Nice? That's all you have to say? He's getting an appointment to West Point. At least, his uncle says he can get him one, and he wants me to *marry* him, Lynette. Isn't that wild?"

"You're only fifteen."

"Well, now I am, but I won't be forever. He's not talking about now. He's talking about when he's an officer. Can't you just see me living on any army base and maybe even overseas somewhere? I'm so excited I could bust." She pranced across the room, stopping to bestow a kiss on Eddie's shaggy head.

Lynette, seeing the kiss, slammed her fist down on the

97

table. The plates she'd just set in place hopped. Eddie glowered at her, then looked back at the televison. Debbi had gone into the bathroom. That did it, Lynette decided. She would take care of Eddie herself.

Two days later, Marie put Penny back into service. "She seems all right," Marie said apologetically to Lynette. "And this little girl is so scared. Penny's the only horse gentle enough for her."

"She's fat," Lynette complained. The child was standing beside her mother as far away from the horses as she could get.

"It's just baby fat," Marie said. "She don't weigh that much."

That evening when Lynette visited Penny in the pasture, the horse was standing by the gate pawing at the ground and whoofing at her foot. Lynette squeezed between the upper and lower bars of the gate and crouched at Penny's feet. The ankle looked swollen, and when Lynette touched Penny's glossy side, it felt sweaty even though it was a cool-enough evening. Immediately, Lynette ran to the woodshed where Marie was pounding a bent bit back into shape.

"Penny's foot's bad, Marie," Lynette said.

Marie dropped what she was doing and went to examine Penny. "Looks like it's infected. Now how did that happen?"

"That's where she stepped on the glass Eddie threw at her."

"It could be a piece of glass's still in there. What we got to do now is remove the shoe and drain the pus, then put on some antibiotic. You'll have to soak the foot in hot water a couple of times a day, Lynette. Then you got to cover the foot with a plastic sack and tie that in place with a burlap bag. She won't need a tetanus injection. Just got one in June. Think you can do all that?"

"Will she be all right?"

"I expect so." Marie stroked Penny reflectively. Then she said, "You send Josh down to help me and you stay up at the house to take care of things there."

"No. I want to be with Penny," Lynette said firmly. She ran for Josh and followed him back to the barn. He put a nose twitch on Penny, a pinching device to distract her from the pain in her hoof so that she wouldn't bolt or kick or try to bite Marie.

"Don't hurt her with that," Lynette protested. "Isn't she in enough pain as is?"

"The nose twitch is just a bother to her while it's on. It's not gonna hurt her, and she'll forget it soon as it's off. Now, don't you give us a hard time, too, Lynny." He held Penny's head with the nose twitch while her eyes rolled wildly and he tried to soothe her with his molasses voice. Lynette stroked Penny's side, choking back whimpers of sympathetic pain as she watched Marie, who had braced Penny's sore foot between her legs and was working on it.

"How's it look?" Josh asked after Marie pried the metal shoe off and cut into the infected part, the soft frog at the back of the hoof.

"She'll feel better when the pus is drained," Marie said.

"Marie's doctoring is good as any vet's," Josh said to Lynette.

"My daddy did all his own vetting. Couldn't afford a real doctor," Marie said.

"Guess your life ain't improved all that much," Josh said ruefully.

"Sure it has, Josh." Marie looked back over her shoulder at him.

Josh grinned at her. "Well, you don't have any more money than you had or any less work."

"I got you," Marie said and Josh looked as satisfied as a well-fed cat.

Watching the interplay of their affection, Lynette forgot Penny for a minute and thought of Jeremy. The kindest thing he'd said to her in weeks had been about the barbecue sauce she'd made for the franks two nights ago.

"You know how to make food taste good," he'd said. "You always did do everything well, even when you were little." But when she'd gazed up at him hoping that he'd decided to love her again, he turned away quickly and asked Josh about the truck's new rattle.

Penny jerked her foot, unbalanced on three legs, and made a strangled noise. "Just about done," Marie said. "Hang on another second."

The only light in the blackness outside when they left the barn was the eerie blue bug light that sizzled as it electrocuted unfortunate insects. "Does a good job, don't it?" Josh said of the bug light as he dropped a heavy arm over Lynette's shoulder. Then he said, "Cheer up, honey, our horse will be fine."

The sizzling bug light and the monotonous zinging of the cicadas and chirping crickets accompanied them as they walked three abreast across the road to the steps. The chorus had a meanacing sound to Lynette's ears.

"Certainly is a dark night," Marie said.

"Clouded over, but warm out. Bet we get some rain tomorrow."

"I'd be glad if it poured," Marie said. "Then my riders'd cancel and I'd get a day off."

"You sure deserve a holiday," Josh said. "Take off tomorrow, anyway, why don't you?"

"No, Josh. The season's too short as is. We still got to feed the horses when no money comes in this winter."

"Gonna have to sell off some horses, anyway, looks like."

"What about the loan?"

"No extension, they said. Figures. I'm thinking of going

back to work at the garage for a while once the summer's over."

"You said you'd never work for them again."

"Just for a few months. It won't kill me."

Lynette shivered as she climbed the stairs behind them. Living was so hard. Hard for Josh and for Marie and for her, too. Only Eddie escaped the pain of not having enough of love or substance. This time he wouldn't get away with it, though. She had a plan of revenge now. Tomorrow, if it didn't rain, or the next day, maybe....

Chapter **13**

Lynette felt like an executioner waiting for the right time to carry out a sentence. She didn't like the feeling, but she was determined to see justice done.

She was in the barn, binding the burlap over the plastic bag that covered the dressing on Penny's foot, when she heard their voices, Eddie's high and Jeremy's bass. The night had been cold with a snap of the coming autumn in it, but Jeremy and Eddie had slept up at their finished fort, anyway. They were walking past the barn on their way home for breakfast. "But I'll be leaving in a few more days," Jeremy was saying.

Lynette led Penny out of the barn in time to see them crossing the road. Their sleeping bags and Jeremy's knapsack humped out on their backs above their narrow hips. From the back, Eddie looked like a small model of Jeremy. He had even copied Jeremy's walk.

"It's time," Lynette told Penny. "Now he'll see he can't get away with everything just because it's you and me."

Penny hobbled off toward the apple tree, swishing her long black tail. Lynette marched to the shed. She surveyed the tools that were suspended from nails and hooks or leaned against the wall. Her eyes moved over the shiny varnish on the pale wooden handle of a new pick, past dirt-crusted shovels and scythes and saws. There were broken tools and pieces of pipe and half-empty cans of paint, buckets and burlap bags. Most carefully kept were the axes which hung between two nails each on the studs of the uninsulated wall. Lynette selected the smallest one. She lifted the slim, steel shaft over her head with both hands and brought the ax head lightly down on a block of wood. She wasn't sure that she was strong enough to destroy Jeremy's handiwork, but she meant to try.

The fort was the only possession Eddie had that wasn't a hand-me-down from his brothers. If she wanted to hurt him as hard as he'd hurt Penny, it had to be the fort.

Carrying the ax, Lynette circled behind the woodpile and plunged into the ravine. It was dry enough to cross now. If she could find the old stump where the deers' path trickled down the mountain, she could climb to the site of the fort, avoiding the bridle paths and any chance of being seen. Something rustled in the leaves ahead of her and scuttled through the underbrush. Woodchuck. The fat brown shape looked like an old shoe. There was the stump. She gripped the ax and climbed, finding the path easily though her hands and cheek got scratched from the vines that snaked across its narrow width. Her determination made her feel strong. At long last, she was doing something herself instead of being a helpless victim.

The fort impressed her when she reached the clearing and stopped to catch her breath. It was small, but it was made of silvery old barn siding and had a window sealed with plastic and an opening that faced a stone-lined fire pit. The coals from last night's fire had been shoveled over with dirt.

She faltered, seeing the care Jeremy had lavished on this building. It would be punishing him, too, if she destroyed it. But he was leaving, anyway, in a few days. She reminded herself of how nasty Eddie had been when Jeremy suggested she come up to share their campfire. Jeremy had wanted to show her what he'd accomplished here, but Eddie had reminded him, "You said no girls in our fort, Jeremy. You said no girls allowed."

"She can just come for the campfire, Eddie."

"I don't like Lynette no more, anyway," Eddie had said.

She would have been hurt, but she understood why he didn't like her. He felt guilty about what he had done to Penny, and rather than be angry at himself, he was angry at her. That was the way he was. He had never accepted the blame for anything in his life.

Inside the fort, they had piled up pine needles to make a soft floor. The only litter was a soup dish, a torn plastic tablecloth and an empty soda-pop can. Experimentally, she lifted the ax and swung it against the left-hand corner post. The post stood firm. She tried harder, swinging against the window area this time, and was rewarded by a splintering of the old siding. Methodically, she kept hacking away at the weakest-looking boards, tossing those that broke out into the clearing. It wasn't easy. She braced herself and whacked as hard as she could, then pried the ends of the boards loose from the posts. She was making so much noise that she expected them to charge into the clearing ready to do battle with her any minute. Hadn't she heard the distant thwack of the hammer going for days while Jeremy was building this place? Tearing it down, hard as the work was, was faster. She wondered if he'd try to repair it for Eddie in the few days he had left. Deliberately, she smashed the boards so that they couldn't be used again. The punishment had to be lasting or it was no good at all.

By the time she had most of the walls broken out, and only the patched metal roof and the framing were left, her arms and back had turned to lead. She could barely lift the ax. Still no one had come. She contemplated the damage. It looked pretty final to her. Where were they? Surely if they were still around the house or barn, or anywhere on the ranch, they would have come to see what was happening. She wanted the confrontation now while she still felt right about what she had done.

Already her mood was changing. Sorrow was creeping in. Why did she always feel sorry for everything she did wrong? Why couldn't she be guilt-free like Eddie? He would hate her, she thought. Suppose Jeremy hated her, too? He might not see it from her point of view. All summer he had refused to understand how it was for her. And he was leaving soon. She wouldn't see him again for so long, maybe forever. And he'd leave angry at her now. She burst into tears. How could the summer she'd had such hopes for have gone so wrong? She would have been better off if he hadn't come at all. Then, at least, she would still have her dream of him to hold against the future.

She shuddered and let the ax slip from her fingers. Why had she done this? Who was she punishing? Eddie was only a bratty little boy who didn't think about the consequences of what he did. He hadn't meant to make Penny lame by throwing that bottle in front of her. And Jeremy couldn't help it if he didn't love her any more. That was her own fault for being unlovable. She hated what she had done. She couldn't imagine how she could have thought it was right. Wearily, she picked up the ax and plodded back to the ranch the easy way along the bridle path. She trudged along with head down, not seeing anything but her sneakered toes moving out one after the other.

Penny was standing above the bench of rock at the top of the pasture with her head up and ears pricked forward as if she were waiting for Lynette. The mare slowly hobbled down the hillside toward the gate, head bobbing and sway-back hanging low. She expected a greeting, but Lynette felt so bad, she ignored Penny. Instead, Lynette crossed the road and climbed up to the house. No one was home. Marie was out on the trails. Debbi was off somewhere, and Jeremy had left a scribbled note on a paper bag on the kitchen table saying he and Eddie had gone to the hardware store with Josh. She put the ax down by the fireplace.

When they asked her why she had done it, she would say, "I did it because Eddie deserved to be punished and nobody else would do it." She would *not* act sorry. She would not act sorry no matter how bad she felt inside. She would stick to her first belief that what she'd done was right. She sighed and went to fill the tub. Maybe if she soaked away her aches, she'd feel better.

She opened the jar of bubble bath Debbi had once given her and scooped out enough to make the surface of the water disappear in a froth of rainbow-tinted bubbles. Sitting in the water, she tried to see how softly she could touch a bubble. Perhaps she could touch one so it wouldn't burst. The cozy memory returned of snuggling against her mother while her mother read to her from *The Little Prince*. A few memories like that were left. Once when Lynette was very small, her teddy bear had disappeared into her toy box and reap-peared, to her enormous relief, when her tears brought her mother on the run. There was the image of her mother's loving smile on Lynette's first day of school, and the scent of her mother's perfume as she enveloped Lynette for a good-night kiss. "My precious," Mother had called her. "My most precious girl."

For a long time Lynette sat in the tub searching her mind, but nothing else came back to her, and the soap bubbles kept bursting no matter how delicately she fingered them.

Chapter **14**

The harsh cawing of vehicles braking nearby and men's voices sharpened by excitement stirred Lynette out of her reverie. What was going on? She pulled the rubber stopper from the drain, got out of the tub and dried herself. In a minute she was dressed and in the living room.

"What's wrong?" she asked Josh, who was just barging down the stairs.

"Oh, there you are. Wanted to make sure you wasn't caught in it. Listen, honey girl, we got us a bad fire on our own land." He shook his head in disbelief and hustled out the door. She followed him but stopped in horror at what she saw. White smoke was rising like a morning mist from the hill near the main riding path. A forest fire! Josh was a member of the volunteer fire department and had fought several fires. He said there was nothing worse in these woods after a dry summer. Within hours, the life's work of a family, acres of valuable timber, half a mountainside could vanish. Sometimes it took days to bring the fire under control. Fires were what the rangers in the mountain-top towers watched for and what other rangers in helicopters patrolled the countryside to spot. As soon as a ranger located a fire, he or she notified the nearest local fire department. Then, as was happening now before her eyes, men would leave their work, grab their fire rakes, hard hats and asbestos gloves, and travel as fast as they could go to as near as they could get to the fire.

A tank truck of water nudged past the cars lining the road. One skinny boy slid his motorcycle to a stop and went running toward the bridle path with a five-gallon backpack of water and a hand pump. Suddenly a column of gray smoke shot up like a stalagmite above the white. Some dry tree had turned into a flaming torch. What could she do to help? No one was around to tell her. Josh had said when fires spread to a barn, it became a trap for any animals inside. She raced down to check the stalls of the horse barn. Any ailing horses penned up there would be safer in the pasture. Nothing could burn a pasture. Or could it? She remembered Josh telling about how even the earth burned sometimes. The black forest mold, full of organic material, would smolder for days, waiting for a breeze to give it enough oxygen to flame up.

Only three horses including Penny were out in the pasture. The rest were on the trail with Marie. Lynette hoped Marie would see the smoke and get back to take charge. And where was Debbi? News would travel fast. If she was anywhere within a radius of a few miles, she would hear about the fire and come home. Jeremy would be up there on the mountain with Josh fighting the fire, no doubt. She hoped Jeremy was wearing his work boots and not his sneakers. Josh said the ground got so hot it melted the soles of sneakers right off. And Eddie, was he up there, too? He could be with Milton, but lately he hadn't been spending much time with Milton. Eddie was too little to be at the fire. If that's were he was, she'd better make him come home.

She filled a plastic jug with water to carry with her and took along an armload of burlap bags. She knew that wetted-down burlap bags could be used to slap against the fire as it crept along the ground.

A jeep bumped up the bridle path with a load of water containers. "Where you going?" the bearded driver asked Lynette. "A fire's no place for little girls."

"I'm looking for my youngest cousin," she said.

"You one of Josh's kids?"

"Yes."

"Come on, then. Hop in."

She could smell the burning pine and the smoldering leaves. As they got closer, the smoke became denser and she started coughing. Dark shapes of men showed up close to the red flames. Two men, well protected by heavy jackets, hard hats, welding gloves and boots, were peeling back the thin carpet of moss and berry bushes with their rakes. Already the landscape had changed so that she could barely recognize where the bridle path had been. The clearing and the evidence of what she had done to Eddie's fort had gone up in smoke. She spotted Jeremy chopping down one of tinder-dry birches whose curly bark burned so well, but she didn't see Eddie.

"Jeremy!" she called. He didn't hear her until she stood beside him. He was puffing and whacking away in double time. "Jeremy, do you know where Eddie is?"

"Lynette! What're you doing here? You crazy? Get back to the house where you'll be safe."

"I'm looking for Eddie."

"He's probably with Josh. Now get home. I don't want to have to worry about you, too."

Silently, she offered him the jug she was carrying. Silently, he took it and glugged down water as if he were parched. "Thanks," he said. As soon as he handed her back

109

the jug, he raised his ax with an anxious glance over his shoulder to check the whereabouts of the fire before he set to work again.

Next, she ran to where the men were spraying water from the hand-held tanks directly on low bushes beset by sparks which had leapfrogged ahead of the advancing flames. Josh was there, directing everybody. He was already so fire-blackened that she only recognized him by his burly shape.

"Josh, have you seen Eddie?" she asked.

"Eddie? He's with Jeremy, isn't he? The little scamp! I told him to get out from underfoot. Maybe he's back at the house. That water you got there?"

The jug was passed around and lifted to the lips of half a dozen thirsty men. A freckle-faced young woman relieved Lynette of the burlap bags. Eddie, Lynette thought nervously. She made a swift tour with her fast-emptying jug down the line of fire fighters who were clearing a bare strip with fire rakes to halt the advancing blaze. Newcomers arrived continuously. The tank truck, horn honking, was still trying to get up the bridle path which was blocked with vehicles. The essential water for the hand pumps and the long hose that the truck carried couldn't get through. In the chaotic scene, Lynette didn't see anybody short enough to be Eddie. It was hot near the fire. She felt the heat of the ground through her sneakers and shivered with fear. Eddie!

At last she dodged around the men and the snarls of equipment and trotted back down the bridle path out of the smoky air. As she ran around the corner of the barn, she heard the sputtering whine of a motor low overhead. It was a whirlybird, probably heading for the fire to drop a load of tools and water.

He wasn't in the house. She checked every room, even the basement. Finally, with trembling fingers, she found and dialed the number of Milton's family motel. No answer.

110

She tried again. Maybe they had all come to help with the fire, too. Then where was Eddie? She chewed the knuckle of her thumb, trying to think. He couldn't have gotten caught in some pocket of brush and—He couldn't be holed up in some rocky crevice surrounded by smoke and—He *had* to be safe. She couldn't endure the thought of Eddie's being in danger. Back down the stairs. Across the road to the barn.

"Eddie!" she shouted. "Eddie, are you in there?" There was no place else to look, but the barn was echoingly empty. "Eddie," she sobbed. "Oh, Eddie."

"I'm up here," came a faint voice.

Relief shook the weight from her shoulders. She felt light and dizzy. "Where are you? I've been looking all over for you."

"What for? I didn't do nothing," he said.

"I thought something might have happened to you." She traced the sound of his voice to the hayloft where they stored the winter supply. It was empty now. She climbed up the rickety wooden ladder nailed to sturdy posts, to the overhead platform which smelled of musty hay. He was sitting next to the wide opening through which the hay bales were escalated into the loft, a lonely little figure looking out toward the mountain side.

"What are you sitting here all by yourself for?" she asked.

"I'm watching my fort burn," he said sadly.

She stepped carefully over the holes in the floor boards and squatted beside him. From the opening in the loft, he could see where his fort had been, all right. From here they had a perfect view of the main bridle path and the clearing beside it, all now breathing black and gray smoke.

"Looks like a volcano," she said. "You feeling bad?"

He nodded.

She put her hand on his. "I'm sorry about your fort," she

said. Then she remembered that before it burned down, she had already destroyed it. "Eddie," she began, but at the same time, he said.

"I guess I'm being punished."

"What for?"

"For being a bad kid. Jeremy said when you're bad, you maybe don't get punished right away, but eventually you do."

"Is that what he told you?"

"He said if I want friends, I got to start being nice to people. He said I should start with you."

She smiled. "Jeremy said that?" she repeated. "That was nice of him. But Eddie, I—" Now she had to confess what she'd done to him.

He's going home in two days," Eddie said gloomily. His eyes were still fixed on the lake of smoke lying amid the green treetops of the mountain side.

"I know....I guess you'll miss him as much as I will— almost....But you have Milton, and school will start soon."

"I hate school, and I don't got Milton no more. He's moving to Florida."

"When?"

"Soon. They went there to pick a place."

She sighed. "Eddie, before your fort burned in the brush fire, I knocked it down with Josh's ax."

"You did?" He looked at her in wide-eyed surprise. "What for?"

"Because you threw that jar and Penny got hurt."

"No, I didn't. That was an accident. Honest, Lynette. I'm not lying. It was an accident this time."

"Well, I thought you threw the jar on purpose so I knocked down your fort. I'm sorry. I'm sorry about Milton, too, for your sake."

"That's O.K." He sounded resigned.

"What is?"

"That you knocked down the fort. I done a lot of stuff to you before."

"You forgive me, then?"

"Sure."

"Oh, Eddie, I forgive you, too." She encircled him with her arms and hugged him against her as she used to when he was little. For a minute he clung to her, nuzzling his head under her chin.

"We better get back to the house and see what we can do to help. Maybe we can make sandwiches or something," she said.

They scrambled out of the loft one after the other. At the open barn door, Lynette noticed the empty field. Empty barn, empty field—where were the horses? Now she had something else to be frantic about. Her body responded with a new surge of energy and she rushed up to the house. This time Marie and Debbi were inside, both busily piling up a huge stack of sandwiches. The smell of perking coffee filled the air.

"Here she is," Debbi said.

"Where have you been, Lynette?" Marie asked.

"Finding Eddie. I thought he was lost at the fire, so I went looking for him."

"Good thing someone keeps track of him," Marie said. "I didn't even think to—"

"I was in the barn," Eddie interrupted.

"Eddie, get me some buckets to carry these sandwiches in," Debbi ordered. "Lynette, you want to carry this food up to the men at the fire, or shall I?"

"I'll go. What happened to the horses?" Lynette asked Marie.

"A farmer took them for us till the danger's past. Nice of him to offer."

"The fire won't spread down to here, will it?" Lynette asked.

"Never can tell with these brush fires."

"What would happen if we lost the barn?" Lynette asked.

"Guess we'd have to shoot ourselves," Marie said cheerfully. Disaster seemed to have lightened her spirits.

"Come on, Lynette. Are you going or not?" Debbi asked.

Lynette picked up the full buckets. She wanted to go back to see how bad things were, anyway. If Josh lost everything—but he couldn't. He'd worked so hard, and Marie worked even harder, and what would happen to Penny? It was a long walk. The smell of burning wood was no longer pleasant, too heavy with acrid smoke. It made her eyes burn. She arrived back at the line of fire fighters choking and coughing and barely able to see.

"Lynette! Over here," a hoarse voice called. It was Josh, looking like a dusty ghost. Only his eyes were alive in the mantle of soot. Men crowded around her, reaching for the sandwiches.

"Prettiest angel of mercy I ever saw," one said.

"This your youngest girl, Josh?

"Youngest and best," Josh said proudly. "She's the one I can count on. Right Lynny?"

She blushed and asked, "Is the fire out?"

"Looks like it might be. Can't be sure yet. We'll have to keep watch on it for a few days.... Remember the fire up by Charlie's camp, Les?"

Now that the flames were out and only smoke charred remains were left, the men could relax. They worked more slowly and stopped to talk about other fires they had fought and the sneaky way some had of reappearing when it seemed they'd been put out. The ranch was saved, Lynette thought. Penny would still have a home and so would she. She wondered if Josh had meant it when he claimed her as his

114

youngest girl and said she was the best. "The one I can count on," he'd said. Did he really think of her that way? She felt so tired all at once that she could barely keep her head up.

"Best get back to the house," Josh told her, "and tell Marie some folks will be stopping by for a drink shortly."

The air didn't seem as bad to Lynette going back, whether because the wind had shifted or because she knew they were safe now, she didn't know. She wanted to creep upstairs and get a nap if they didn't need her for anything else right now. And had Josh really meant what he said about her? She thought fondly of Eddie. He wasn't such a bad kid, kind of cute and funny, actually. Maybe they could build another fort together somewhere this fall after Milton was gone and Jeremy left, when it was just Eddie and her alone together. Maybe that would be a fun thing to do after school in the late afternoons.

Chapter **15**

The sound of Josh's snarling voice woke Lynette. She sat up in bed and listened. Josh and Jeremy. What was Josh angry about? Anxiously, she rolled to her feet, glanced at her grimy face in the mirror and left the bedroom without doing anything about it.

"People been killed fighting fires in these woods plenty of times. Let me tell you, they ain't nothing to take lightly. People get sent to jail for less than starting one of these fires." Josh was planted in the middle of the living room, talking at Jeremy who was sitting at the kitchen table having his hand bandaged by Debbi.

"I'm certainly not taking the fire lightly, Josh," Jeremy defended himself. "Remember me? I was the one got my hand burned."

"Yeah, you got a little blistered. Too bad you got careless this afternoon. Maybe you got careless early this morning, too."

"Hey, what are you saying? You mean, you think I had something to do with that fire? Eddie and I left a clean campsite this morning. It was properly taken care of."

"Wonder what started that fire, then."

"I don't know. It's a puzzle, all right."

"Puzzle, huh? I give you three guesses." Josh's voice had wound tight with anger. "It wasn't lightning because we didn't have none. The other two major causes of forest fires are cigarettes and untended campfires."

"If you're blaming me, come out and say it. I don't smoke and neither does Eddie, so it had to be the campfire according to you, huh?"

"Think about it, Mr. Big Time Boy Scout. Who was it, if not you?"

Jeremy pulled his hand away from Debbi's bandaging and stood up to face Josh. "I shoveled dirt over it just like you're supposed to to put it out."

"Yeah, dirt with plenty of dry leaves and twigs in it, I bet. I know. You do everything you're supposed to. Like you come here to work so you can spend time with that little girl up there who'd held you up like her personal savior all these years, and who do you spend your time with? Debbi here, who's got more boys yapping at her heels than she knows what to do with already, and Eddie, who don't need you to play with."

"I worked hard for you this summer, Josh." Jeremy's face was red but his voice was controlled.

"Yeah, you did," Josh admitted. "But you neglected that little girl something shameful."

"Josh," Marie said. "It's not your business."

"All I'm pointing out is he's not so perfect, Marie. He's the only one *could've* started that fire, and he ought to own up to it and take the consequences."

"You itching to haul me off to jail for commiting arson, Josh?" Jeremy asked.

Abruptly, the horror that had been growing in Lynette as she listened burst and the burning knowledge of who was responsible for the fire poured over her. She cringed. Her impulse was to run and hide, so great was her fear of what Josh would do when he found out who really had set the fire. but it was Jeremy who had been accused, her Jeremy. She couldn't let him be punished in her place.

With an act of will, she forced herself to step around the curve and into view. Her voice was so strained that she didn't know if they heard her when she said, "It wasn't Jeremy's fault."

But they all looked up, including Eddie who was sitting on the cushions on the floor with his back to the TV.

"I did it," she said. "I started the fire." Her body began trembling so violently that her teeth chattered.

"You don't have to stick up for Jeremy," Josh said to her. "He's big enough to defend himself."

"It was me," she said, and shaky as she was, she began to explain. "I went up to the fort after they left it this morning, and I broke it down with your little steel ax. I banged the walls down and left the broken pieces all over. Some must have fallen in the fireplace."

"I thought I heard hammering, but I just figured they were still working on the place," Marie murmured in the silence.

"*You* knocked down the fort?" Debbi asked as if she couldn't believe it.

"I was punishing Eddie for throwing the glass jar at Penny. I thought he did it on purpose, but he didn't " She looked at Josh, who was frowning at her without saying a word. "Please, Uncle Josh, don't send me to jail," she begged. "I've never done anything bad before. I know it was awful, but I didn't mean to set a fire. If you have to send me away, please don't send me anyplace bad."

"What's the matter with you, are you crazy?" Debbi asked her. "Josh," Debbi said, "tell this crazy kid now that you're not sending her to jail."

"I can't believe Lynny'd knock that fort down," Josh said wonderingly.

"Don't send Lynette to jail, Josh," Eddie piped up. "It was all my fault. She got mad at me because I wasn't nice. I do mean things to her all the time. Like I put ice cubes in her bed and hide her books and put glue in her hairbrush, and I wrecked her sweater."

"She did it 'cause she was mad at *you*, Eddie?" Josh asked, trying to get it straight.

"Yeah, but now I'm gonna be nice."

"You are, huh?"

"Jeremy says I gotta be nice or nobody's gonna like me."

Josh gave Jeremy an embarrassed look. "Well, Boy Scout, I guess you are good for something. I apologize for taking out after you like I did."

"That's O.K., Josh. I'm just glad it *wasn't* me started that—" Jeremy caught himself and looked guiltily at Lynette, who was still staring at Josh and waiting.

"Ah, nobody started it," Josh decided. "It was just a gosh-darned accident. Right, Marie?"

"Sounds that way," Marie agreed.

"Come on over here, Lynette," Josh said. "You got nothing to look so scared about. The fire wasn't much. Didn't do hardly no damage at all." He held his hand out to her.

She didn't understand. She'd given him all the excuse to get rid of her that he needed. "Aren't you going to send me away?" she asked.

"Send you away? What for? Every kid makes mistakes. Anyway, we're your family, Lynny. I can't send you anywhere. You got to leave us on your own when you're ready, like the boys did."

She began to cry, great gulping sobs of relief. He gathered her into a rough embrace against his solid chest. She buried her face in his shirt, which smelled of smoke and sweat.

"Josh wouldn't hold anything against you no matter what you did, Lynette," Marie said. "He thinks the world of you, and he loves you. We all do."

That brought on a fresh rush of tears. Josh patted Lynette's back. "Don't cry, honey. I can't stand hearing you cry. Stop it now. You didn't do nothing. And even if you did, you're still my sweet little girl."

"Listen to him," Debbi said. "He's gonna break down and cry, too, if you don't stop, Lynny."

Lynette got control of herself and drew away from her hiding place at Josh's armpit. Everyone began to laugh. "What's so funny?" she wanted to know.

"Go look at yourself in the mirror," Debbie said. "You got a piece of coal instead of a nose stuck in the middle of your face. Josh's covered with soot."

Lynette washed her face and, at Josh's urging, got out of the bathroom so that he could soak off the effects of the fire in a tub of hot water. By the time she reentered the living room, they were all occupied with usual suppertime activities. Eddie and Jeremy were watching TV. Debbi and Marie were cutting up salad. They all looked the same as they always did to Lynette, but she felt different. For the first time, she was not teetering on the outside edge of the family, gauging their acceptance of her. For the first time, she had no doubt of her welcome. She was one of them. She belonged.

Chapter 16

Josh had told Jeremy to be ready to leave at ten. They'd drive to the bus station in Lake George Village then, but first, Josh had work to do. Jeremy had stayed in the house that morning. He'd packed his belongings and was helping Lynette clean up the kitchen after the chaos of do-it-yourself breakfasts was over. Debbi had already cheerfully kissed Jeremy good-by and gone off shopping for school clothes with a girlfriend. Eddie was down the road visiting Milton, who was back from Florida temporarily.

"We still have half an hour till I leave. Want to take a walk?" Jeremy asked Lynette when they had finished cleaning up.

"I have to bring a carrot out to Penny. We could walk out to the pasture."

"You and that horse," Jeremy said. "I think you love that animal more than any human around here."

"No, I don't," she said.

"You don't, huh? I suppose you love Eddie more?"

He was teasing, but she answered him seriously, "I love Eddie and Uncle Josh and Debbi and Marie more than any horse—even Penny."

"Well, that's a surprise. I'd never guessed that," he said.

"I've always loved them, Jeremy. I just didn't know they loved me back."

"And now you know?"

"Yes." She had given them good reason to reject her. She had done a destructive thing by wrecking Eddie's fort and causing that fire, but they hadn't turned against her. Never before had she felt so secure in the knowledge that they loved her. She had been bad and been forgiven.

They walked down the stone steps for the last time and crossed the road, heading for the pasture. All Jeremy's belongings were in the green backpack strapped over his shoulders.

"I've got to tell you something, Lynette," he said. "You were right. I did only come here this summer because I couldn't find any place better to go. By the time I broke up with my girl, it was too late to get a job outside Boston, and I didn't think I could stand staying home and maybe bumping into her at our usual hangouts. It really does a job on a guy's ego to get dumped like that.... So, anyway, I came here without thinking about how it would be for you. I remembered you as a little girl, and I cared about what happened to you, but I never thought that you'd—"

"Expect you to really love me," she finished for him.

"Yeah.... That shook me. And you're getting close to being a woman now. And a child who turned out to be almost a woman who turned out to love me was more than I could handle."

"I know," she said.

"You understand?"

"I do now, Jeremy." She smiled a trembling smile at him.

"Then we're still friends?"

Her smile stretched beyond the tremble and she looked him full in the eyes. "I hope so. Oh, yes!" she said. She

122

loved him so much, and he didn't love her back, not the way she had dreamed. But she could live with that now.

"I'm sorry I messed up," he said. "Maybe some other summer—"

"Don't keep saying good-by, Jeremy," she said coolly. "You want to give Penny her carrot?"

Jeremy opened the gate and offered Lynette his arm in a half humorous gesture of courtesy. She slipped her hand through the crook of his elbow, and they walked together over the tufted hummocks and rocks, bumping hips companionably, to the tree where Penny stood watching them. The warm, sympathetic look of the mare's dark-centered, brown eyes nearly made Lynette cry. Jeremy was leaving. Who knew when she'd see him again? Jeremy extended the carrot and Penny took it gently from his fingers, wrinkling back her lip over her big teeth. The brash horn of Josh's truck summoned them.

Lynette turned to go, but Jeremy caught her arm. "Hey, I'm gonna miss you," he said. He grazed the side of her forehead with his lips. "Write me?"

"You write me first and I'll answer," she said boldly, the way Debbi would have spoken. This time it worked.

"Fair enough," he said.

And then some other summer, she thought—No, she wouldn't count on that. Instead, she'd build different dreams for herself and she'd keep growing up. Then maybe, some other summer, if they met again, it might just happen that he *would* begin to love her. The horn blared impatiently. It could happen that way, she thought. Among all the endless possibilities, that was one. But she wasn't going to count on it. She didn't need to anymore.

"Let's go," she said. She ran toward the gate and he followed.